He named  been making before. Only a fool would turn down this opportunity, but then again, working with Devlyn Wolff would not be easy. He was charming and outrageously handsome and had a wicked sense of humor... All qualities that were destined to make a woman like Gillian fall into infatuation at the very least.

And she was pretty sure she wasn't imagining the sexual vibe between them. What was alarming was that if she succumbed, not only did she endanger yet another good job, but she risked getting her heart broken.

"I'm a businessman. And despite your hang-ups, I'm not offering you this job because of something that happened when we were kids."

He could deny it all he wanted, but she was almost one hundred percent sure that Devlyn was the kind of man who needed to even the scales. This was his way of assuaging his guilt over the past.

Still, who was she to turn down a boon because of his screwed-up motives?

"I'll do it," she said. "When do I start?"

Dear Reader,

Before I turned to writing full-time, I taught elementary school for about fifteen years…half of that time in kindergarten and the other half in second grade. I have wonderful memories of smiling faces and happy giggles. When you teach little children, you experience what it means to have someone hang on your every word and soak up knowledge with enthusiasm and eager interest.

But the job is not easy. Despite the challenges, frustrations and disappointments, most of the teachers I know go to work each day determined to do their best in circumstances that are not always ideal. To me, my friends are heroes…making a difference, changing lives in ways so immense the impact cannot be measured.

I hope you enjoy Gillian's story…and Devlyn's. Love really does conquer all. Just ask a teacher.…

Happy reading,

Janice Maynard

JANICE MAYNARD

THE MAID'S DAUGHTER

HARLEQUIN®

entertain, enrich, inspire™

Recycling programs
for this product may
not exist in your area.

ISBN-13: 978-0-373-73195-4

THE MAID'S DAUGHTER

Copyright © 2012 by Janice Maynard

www.Harlequin.com

Printed in U.S.A.

JANICE MAYNARD

came to writing early in life. When her short story *The Princess and the Robbers* won a red ribbon in her third-grade school arts fair, Janice was hooked. She holds a B.A. from Emory and Henry College and an M.A. from East Tennessee State University. In 2002 Janice left a fifteen-year career as an elementary teacher to pursue writing full-time. Her first love is creating sexy, character-driven, contemporary romance. She has written for Kensington and NAL, and now is so very happy to also be part of the Harlequin Books family—a lifelong dream, by the way!

Janice and her husband live in beautiful east Tennessee in the shadow of the Great Smoky Mountains. She loves to travel and enjoys using those experiences as settings for books.

Hearing from readers is one of the best perks of the job! Visit her website, www.janicemaynard.com, or email her at JESM13@aol.com. And of course, don't forget Facebook (www.facebook.com/JaniceMaynardReaderPage). Find her on Twitter at www.twitter.com/JaniceMaynard and visit all the men of Wolff Mountain at www.wolffmountain.com.

For all my teacher buddies
in the Sevier County School System—
you know who you are! It was an honor
and a pleasure to work beside you year after year.
Thanks for your dedication *in the trenches*. :)

One

Wet yellow leaves clung to the rain-slick, winding road. Devlyn Wolff took the curves with confidence, his vintage Aston Martin hugging the pavement despite the windswept October day. Dusk had fallen. He switched on his headlights, drumming his fingers on the steering wheel in rhythm to the hard-rock oldie blasting from his Bose speakers.

No matter how fast he drove, he couldn't outrun his restlessness. He'd been on Wolff Mountain for a week, and already his father and his Uncle Vic were driving him batty. They had installed him as CEO of Wolff Enterprises two years ago, supposedly with their full trust at his back, but they loved playing Monday-morning quarterback.

It was easier when Devlyn was in Atlanta, ensconced in his fancy-ass office. Then the two Wolff patriarchs could only harass him via email and the phone. But giving up control of the company had been hard for them, and Devlyn did his best to make them feel connected, hence his frequent trips home.

His tires squealed as they spun slightly, seeking a connection with the rural highway. Devlyn knew these back roads intimately. He'd learned to drive here, had wrapped his first car around a tree not two miles up the road. For that reason alone, he eased off the gas.

At that instant, the glare of oncoming headlights blinded him as a car rounded the upcoming curve uncomfortably close to his lane. Devlyn tensed, gripping the wheel and wrestling his vehicle into submission. The other car wasn't so lucky.

Devlyn cursed as the little navy Honda spun past him, its white-faced driver momentarily visible, before the small sedan slid off the road and smashed into a telephone pole. Devlyn eased to a halt on the narrow shoulder and bounded out of the car, his heart punching in his chest as he dialed 911. By the time he hung up and reached the car, the driver was already opening her door. Air bags had deployed in the crumpled vehicle. The woman staggered to her feet, wiping ineffectually at a trickle of blood on her cheek. Even in the waning light of day, he could see a reddish mark on her cheekbone.

He grabbed for her as her knees gave out. "Steady," he said. The ground was the closest surface, unfortunately. She went down gracefully, like butter melting on a hot day. His arm was around her, but the gravel slope beneath their feet was uneven. It was all he could do to keep both of them from sliding down the embankment.

Crouching beside her, he pushed her hair from her face. "You okay?"

Her teeth were chattering. "You nearly killed me."

"Me?" His brows shot up in sync with his temper. "Lady, you crossed the center line."

Her chin lifted slightly. "I'm a very safe driver."

Glancing over his shoulder, he cursed. "Not from where I'm standing."

She shivered hard, and he realized with chagrin that this wasn't the place for such a conversation. "Your car is toast," he said. "The nearest ambulance service is forty-five minutes away at least. It will save time if we meet them in the next valley. I'll take you."

"So says the big bad wolf."

"Excuse me?"

She managed a smile, though her lips were blue. "Devlyn Wolff. What brings you here from Atlanta?"

"Do I know you?" He was acquainted with most of the people in this small section of the Blue Ridge Mountains, but occasionally someone new moved into the area. Then again, something about this woman was familiar.

"Not really," she said. Her nose wrinkled. "I'm getting wet."

He'd been so caught up in worrying about her that he hadn't noticed the rain. They were only half a mile from the driveway to Wolff Mountain, and thus his doctor cousin's clinic, but Jacob was out of town.

Grinding his teeth in frustration, Devlyn glanced at his watch. He had a late dinner meeting with a powerful, important investor in Charlottesville in less than two hours. But he couldn't possibly walk away from a woman who might be seriously injured. Wolff Mountain was isolated for a reason, but at times like this, the remoteness of his childhood home was a curse.

"Let me carry you to my car. You may be hurt more badly than you realize." Even as he said the words out loud, he winced inwardly. *Saint Devlyn to the rescue.* He wasn't a saint—far from it—but he had an unfortunate penchant for rescuing strays, be they animal or human. A tendency that had bitten him in the ass more than once.

She stood up, wavering only slightly. "That's very kind of you. But weren't you headed somewhere?"

Shrugging, he rose to his feet, as well. "I can reschedule."
And potentially lose twenty million dollars. He'd been coaxing
this particular venture capitalist into trusting him for almost
a year. So the moment was likely lost. But money was just
money, and he'd seen enough sports accidents in his college
days to realize that head injuries were not to be taken lightly.

If he could meet up with the paramedics quickly enough,
he might still be able to make his appointment. The woman
clearly knew who he was, so presumably she trusted him
not to be an ax murderer. He scooped her into his arms and
carried her toward his car. Her token protest was feeble. The
tremors that shook her slender body were undoubtedly a de-
layed reaction to the crash. She might have been killed.

His arms tightened around her, his breath hitching as
for a split second he imagined what could have happened.
Thank God she survived the impact. Her wet hair and clothing smelled of roses, an old-fashioned scent that suited her
somehow.

Once, he stumbled slightly, and her hand gripped a fist-
ful of his shirt, her fingernails digging into his skin. For a
second he flashed on an entirely inappropriate scenario that
involved him and her. Naked. In his bed.

He shook his head. Weird. Too weird.

He deposited her gently into the passenger seat and jogged
back to retrieve her purse. When he slid behind the wheel
and looked at her, she grimaced. "I'm not going to keel over,
I promise. The air bags did their job."

"Maybe so, but you look like hell."

Her jaw dropped. "Well, it just goes to show…"

"What do you mean?" He eased the car out onto the road.

"All the tabloids call you a billionaire playboy, but if that's
your slick line with women, they've got it all wrong."

"Very funny." He peered through the windshield and upped
the defroster. It was completely dark now. He turned off the

music, not sure if his tastes would soothe a woman who had been knocked around in an accident. The car was silent except for the swish of the wipers.

His passenger ignored him, her body nestled into the soft leather seat. Though she seemed relaxed, her arms were wrapped tightly around her waist.

A memory kept nagging at his brain. Something to do with this slight, mousy female. But try as he might, it wouldn't come into focus.

She sighed deeply. "I hate inconveniencing you. You could drop me at my mother's house."

"Is she home?"

"Not at the moment. But she'll be back in the morning. She drove down to Orlando to visit my Aunt Tina." She paused and winced when the car hit a bump. "I'm sure I'm fine."

"Don't be ridiculous. We Wolffs may have a reputation for being reclusive, but we're pretty tame when it comes down to it."

Her muttered retort was lost in the squeal of his brakes when he stopped short to avoid hitting a deer. The animal froze, peering at them through the windshield, before bounding into the woods.

Devlyn covered the remaining distance to the main highway and up over the small gap that led to a more populated area to the east, refusing to admit, even to himself, that he was rattled. "Not long now."

"I'm surprised you drive your own car. I thought the Wolff entourage relied on limos."

"I'm a control freak. I like taking the wheel."

Maybe he was imagining it, but he was picking up on some mixed vibes from his damsel in distress. Hostility, perhaps… as if she really did blame him for the accident. But even more than that, an odd intimacy, as if she knew more about him than he did about her. Devlyn was disconcerted. He was accustomed to women tucking their phone numbers into his pocket, not looking down their noses at him.

With one last call to 911, he flagged down the approaching ambulance and pulled off the road. He set the parking brake with a jerk. Before he could come around to offer assistance, his mystery lady was out of the car and heading toward the man and woman in uniform.

Damn her stubborn hide. He loped after her. If the professionals decided she needed to go to the hospital, Devlyn was off the hook.

In deference to the worsening weather, the responders left the gurney inside and had the woman stretched out by the time Devlyn approached. "Do you think it's serious?" he asked, speaking to the medic at the back of the vehicle.

She gave him that look reserved for clueless family members. "We'll know in a little bit."

The man inside bent over the patient, checking vitals. He began asking a string of questions. But one snagged Devlyn's attention right off. *Name?*

The mystery woman's eyes met Devlyn's across the space of several feet. She hesitated.

The question came a second time, more forcefully as the man frowned. *Name?*

Devlyn saw her inner struggle, and her capitulation. "Gillian Carlyle," she said clearly. Was that a glint of defiance Devlyn saw in her gaze?

Gillian Carlyle. Why did that sound so familiar? He didn't know this woman, did he?

While the medical exam continued, Devlyn analyzed the puzzle. Gillian's looks were unexceptional. Medium brown hair, darker brown eyes, pale skin, an angular figure. The cream angora sweater she wore along with a brown corduroy skirt and knee-length boots were not in any way provocative. She wasn't his type, not at all. So he knew they hadn't dated in some far-distant adolescent past. Yet for some reason, he was intrigued.

Finally, she was allowed to sit up. "Thank you," she said quietly. "I'm feeling much better now."

The ambulance driver began putting away all the equipment, addressing Devlyn over Gillian's head. "She told me you were the Good Samaritan who stopped to help her. Can you drive her home? She's gonna be okay. Lots of bumps and bruises, though. Make sure she's not alone tonight in case anything crops up that we missed. She should see her doctor for a follow-up visit tomorrow."

Devlyn groaned inwardly. Even if he dashed back up the mountain and took the chopper, he'd never make it now. "Sure," he said, with a smile that felt like a grimace. "I'd be glad to." In the boardroom, he had no trouble acting like a bastard. Not so much in real life.

He watched Gillian deal with the necessary evil of insurance info. Then he shepherded her back to the car, his arm around her narrow waist. Her bone structure was slender, though she was fairly tall. She fit against his shoulder as if she had been created for just that spot. In the flashing lights from the ambulance he could see that she was dangerously near the point of exhaustion.

How in God's name could he simply drop her off at a deserted house in her condition? "Is there anyone you can call to stay with you tonight? A friend? A neighbor?"

"No. But I'll be fine." She turned her head away from him.

He tucked her into the car and kicked the heat on full blast. If his big body was chilled, she must be freezing. Consigning his last hope of making the business meeting to hell, he sighed. "I'm taking you to Wolff Mountain. We have enough guest rooms for a small army. No one will bother you, but you'll have help close by if you need it. I'll call a tow truck in the morning and we'll see about your car."

She half turned to face him, her body visibly shaking. Moisture glittered in her eyes. "You don't even remember who I am, do you? Even after you heard me say my name. Take me home, Devlyn. I don't belong on your mountain."

And just like that, a memory clicked…

Devlyn recalled the day with painful clarity. It was the first anniversary of the terrible tragedy that had torn the Wolff family apart. On that particular sunny afternoon, Devlyn's father and uncle had insisted that their six combined children help scatter two urns of ashes over a newly planted rose garden on the side of the mountain.

For Devlyn, the process was gruesome and confusing. As soon as he was able, he fled to the secret cave that had become solace at his new home. A girl appeared from nowhere it seemed, staring at him with pity, pity he loathed.

"I'm sorry your mother died," she said. Her long, caramel-brown hair had been plaited into two identical braids that hung forward over her narrow shoulders.

Devlyn was embarrassed and humiliated. Boys didn't cry, especially not in front of girls. He ran a hand across his nose and was further mortified to see a smear of snot. "I hated her," he said abruptly. "I'm glad she's gone."

The girl's long-lashed eyes widened. "Don't be stupid," she said. "You can't hate your mother. She was beautiful. Like a princess. My mother lets me go into Mr. Wolff's bedroom sometimes when she's cleaning…if I'm really good. I love to look at Mrs. Wolff's picture on the wall." She held out her hand. "Here… I made you a card."

Devlyn's desperate anger swelled, determined to end this encounter. "You're not allowed," he shouted, knocking the small folded construction paper out of her hand. "Not anymore. This is my mountain, and you don't belong here. Go home."

Her face crumpled. He felt as if he had kicked one of the

new puppies that lived down at the stables. The silent misery on her delicate features only made him madder. "Go," *he screamed. "Go away."*

Devlyn felt anew the weight of guilt and remorse. For over two decades, he had carried the burden of knowing he had hurt a young girl with his hateful words. Now here she was. As if fate had given him a second chance.

He *could* pretend he didn't know her...could text a late arrival to his much-anticipated appointment and drop Gillian as quickly as possible. But his own cruelty stared him in the face. "Gillian," he said slowly. "Gillian Carlyle. It's been a long time."

Two

A quarter of a century had passed since Gillian had tried, in her own clumsy way, to extend sympathy to a hurting boy. But the passage of time had in no way dulled the memory of how she felt that day when the little rich kid kicked metaphorical sand in her face.

What made it worse was that she knew, even then, that he was right. Gillian's mother scrubbed toilets for a living. The Wolffs were richer than God. It was the first time Gillian had fully understood a difficult truth about the haves and the have-nots.

"It took you long enough," she said. The snarky retort was unfair, but she wasn't in a mood to be conciliatory. Though she no longer carried a chip on her shoulder, it had taken time and maturity to help her see that the Carlyles were every bit as happy as the wealthy Wolff clan in their fortress on the mountain. Maybe more so.

As a child, she had been tormented. She begged her mother

not to make Gillian go to work with her. But Doreen Carlyle had few options. Child care was not only expensive, but in a little wide-place-in-the-road like Burton, it was nonexistent.

Gillian was forced to see Devlyn occasionally, though each of them tried to ignore the other. Things were better when school started. Doreen put her young daughter on a bus before sunup for the long ride to the nearest consolidated school. And by the time Gillian returned home, her mother was finished with her shift at Wolff Castle, as the locals called it.

Gillian jerked herself out of the past, glad of the darkness that hid her turbulent emotions. She straightened in her seat. "It's really okay to take me to my mother's house. I promise I'll call someone if I start to feel worse."

It was the presence of a Wolff in the car, not her accident, that was responsible for the rapid pace of her heartbeat. Devlyn was a big man, broad through the shoulders and tall. The scent of his aftershave made her think of thick fir-tree forests and lumberjacks in flannel shirts, though the comparison was ludicrous.

Devlyn was an astute businessman, a shark in the turbulent world of financial greed. Despite the fact that her wits had been partially addled after the accident, she'd still been aware of his sartorial perfection, though he was perhaps a tad rumpled and sported a five-o'clock shadow.

He was the de facto ruler of the kingdom and, in that moment, Gillian hated him. When had he ever had to work for anything? When had he ever had to worry about money? Other than his mother's death years ago, admittedly a terrible loss, when had he ever known true hardship?

That wasn't fair perhaps. The Wolffs generously supported many worthy charities. Perhaps that chip on her shoulder still lingered as a splinter in her heart. And maybe she was manufacturing grievances in order to avoid admitting how much she was attracted to him.

Even as a teenager, on the few occasions she actually saw him, he had been breathtakingly handsome. Blunt, masculine features. Thick black hair with the sheen of a raven's wing. A white smile that flashed often. And a tough, honed body that exuded strength and confidence.

Little had changed except that now he was a man and not a boy. He had filled out, lost the slightly clumsy awkwardness of puberty. His gait was strong and sure, his movements sleek as the panthers that once roamed these hills.

He shot her a glance as he once again turned onto the road that led up to the entrance to Wolff Mountain. "I'm not arguing about this, Gillian. I'm sorry I didn't recognize you right off. But you have to admit that you've changed."

Did his gaze linger on her chest? Or was that her imagination? Surely not. She might be all tingly with perfectly natural feminine longing for a man who exuded an earthy sex appeal, but to think he had any interest in her was ridiculous.

Her instinct was to shoot back with a smart-ass comment about kidnapping, but she bit her tongue. Devlyn's mother and aunt had been snatched off a busy Charlottesville street, held for ransom and later killed. Kidnapping was not something to be joked about.

She shifted restlessly. Already her battered body bloomed with myriad aches and throbs. The paramedics had recommended an anti-inflammatory, but though she had some ibuprofen in her purse, she had nothing with which to wash them down. Suddenly, the idea of staying alone overnight held little appeal.

At the guardhouse Devlyn sketched a wave and waited for the huge mechanized metal gate to retract. Soon they were heading up the winding drive that served to isolate the Wolff clan from intruders.

She sighed deeply. "I'm not sure this is a good idea. I don't want to intrude on your family."

"They won't even know you're around…unless you want company."

"Why don't you have your own place here?"

He must have picked up on the faint, unintended criticism in her tone. "As you've already mentioned, I live in Atlanta," he said stiffly. "When I visit, I usually stay up in the big house with my dad and uncle." He paused. "If it would make you more comfortable, we can stay at Jacob's place. He and his wife won't care."

"He's the one married to the movie star, right? Ariel Dane?"

"Yep. She's a sweetheart."

Gillian's spirits plunged to a new low. The gorgeous, sexy Wolff men had their pick of models, heiresses and celebrities. It wasn't simply a matter of money. It was a lifestyle.

"I don't think it would be appropriate for the two of us to spend the night alone," she said, regretting the prim stuffiness in her words as soon as they left her mouth.

Devlyn snorted, and tried to pretend it was a cough. "I promise to be on my best behavior," he said, irony in every syllable. "But if it makes you feel more comfortable, we'll stay at the big house."

"Thank you."

By the time they pulled up in front of the massive structure that looked like Cinderella's castle on steroids, Gillian had trouble getting out of the car. Devlyn took her arms and gently pulled her to her feet. "Poor Gillian," he said.

The soft croon in his deep voice made her tremble. She was unable to protest when he scooped her up and carried her into the house. Striding through darkened hallways, he set a course for a back staircase that led to the second floor. Thankfully, they met no one on the way.

Devlyn paused before a half-open doorway. "This is my room. There's an adjoining suite with a door you can lock.

But if you need assistance during the night, you can text me or call me and I'll get you anything you need."

How about you, Devlyn Wolff? In the buff. Sliding on top of me and...

Her breath caught in her throat. She was suffering the effects of a long dry spell in the sex department. That's why she wanted to nibble his throat despite the fact that she felt as if she'd been run over by the proverbial truck. Proximity and deprivation. Simple explanations for the electric connection she felt to a man who was in no way an appropriate object of her fantasies.

Well, yes...for fantasy...in the abstract. But not at all healthy or practical to imagine him...and her...together... Oh, Lord. Her thighs clenched and her nipples tightened. She prayed he didn't notice.

His bed was neatly made. But a pair of jeans hung haphazardly over the back of an armchair, and a paperback crime novel lay upside down on the mahogany nightstand.

"I'm sure I'll be fine," she croaked.

Without acknowledging her comment, he took her, still in his arms, through the doorway into a room that was almost as large as his but was decorated in more feminine tones. Ever so gently, he set her on her feet. "Bathroom's through there. I'll see if I can round you up some clean clothes, and I'll call Jacob to see what medicine you can take."

Before she could catch her breath, he was gone.

She hobbled into the luxurious bathroom and stared in the mirror. If she'd had any illusions about her comparison to the female companionship usually enjoyed by Wolff men, they were shattered decisively by her reflection. Even on a good day, she didn't stand out in a crowd. Right now, she looked ghastly.

Stripping out of her rain-damp clothes, she adjusted the water and stepped into the shower. The hot pelting spray hurt in a good way, the steamy warmth penetrating her bones. Already, bruises were showing up on her too-pale skin. She'd taught a summer-school session instead of going to the beach with her girlfriends, and look where that had gotten her.

Knowing she didn't have the strength or the will to blow-dry her hair, and since she'd shampooed it the night before, she was careful to keep it from getting wet. As she stepped out of the shower and was drying off, a knock on the door startled her so much that she dropped her towel. "Don't come in," she cried, scrambling to cover her indecent bits.

A chuckle was her only answer. The door eased open a scant foot. One long-fingered, tanned hand reached in holding soft, clean clothes. The items landed on the counter with a muted plop, and the hand withdrew.

Gillian scurried forward and locked the knob with what sounded like a gunshot-loud click. She was pretty sure she heard Devlyn laugh again. The bounty he had provided included a set of lounging pj's...the kind you see in the Neiman Marcus catalog, the kind only rich women owned and wore.

The fabric was incredibly soft and warm, though not thick...some sort of cashmere blend. The cinnamon shade flattered her hair and added a snippet of color to her washed-out complexion.

She put on naughty silk panties that most likely belonged to Devlyn's sister, Annalise, then slipped into the top and pants. Devlyn hadn't added a bra. Gillian's own underwear tended toward cotton practicality. The new undies made her aware of the place between her thighs that throbbed as insistently as her injuries. And her breasts rubbed sensuously against the velvetlike fabric.

When she exited the bathroom, barefooted, she stopped short. Devlyn stood by the fireplace where a fire crackled with blissful heat. He had dragged a small table near the hearth, and it was set with an array of dishes. Her stomach growled audibly.

He held out a hand. "Come eat. And Jacob said you can double the usual dose of over-the-counter pain meds. If he were here, he could give you something stronger."

Shyness engulfed her. She had to force herself to approach him. "That will be fine. Don't worry about me."

He held out her chair, his arm brushing her shoulder as she sat down. "I can't seem to help it," he said wryly.

The carpet beneath her feet was soft as a cloud. She curled her toes into it and took a deep breath. "I know you didn't cause my accident," she said, looking up at him through downcast lashes. "I was just in a bad mood. I'm sorry."

He sat down as well, and poured each of them a cup of tea. The juxtaposition of his big, manly hands against the wafer-thin china teapot was incongruous and alarming. How could she keep him at arm's length if he didn't remain in the box she had labeled "spoiled rich philanderer."

She didn't want to like Devlyn Wolff. Not at all.

He took her lack of enthusiasm the wrong way. "It's herbal tea," he said. "No caffeine. But I can get you coffee if you'd rather have it."

Picking up the lovely ivory cup scattered with blue forget-me-nots, she shook her head. "I prefer the tea. Thank you."

He had fixed a tray of sandwiches as well—tiny, slightly ragged squares of white bread with the crusts removed. Peanut butter and honey.

Her whole body tensed. "Why did you make these?" she asked, her insides in a knot.

Devlyn shrugged, his expression moody. "As a penance, I guess. I remember watching you eat them in the kitchen when your mother was on her lunch break. I was jealous, you know. My mother never cooked anything."

Gillian didn't know what to say to that. No one *cooked* peanut butter. But she understood what he was telling her.

He waved a hand. "You need to eat something so the medicine won't upset your stomach."

Too late. The accident, this intimate tête-à-tête, Devlyn's unexpected domesticity…all of it had her in turmoil.

Mute and uncomfortable, she picked up a piece of sandwich, chewed and swallowed. The familiar tastes from her childhood opened a floodgate of memories. His hostility. Her feelings of inferiority. The emotions were as sharp and crisp as yesterday.

Yet he spoke of penance.

"You have nothing for which to apologize," she said slowly, eyeing him over the rim of her teacup. "You were hurting. We were both children." She didn't insult him by pretending not to understand what he was talking about. Their youthful confrontation in the cave all those years ago had clearly bothered him as well as her.

Devlyn wolfed down five mini-sandwiches to her two, and drained three cups of tea. For some reason, she was infinitely fascinated by the play of muscles in his throat as he swallowed. Everything about him was intensely virile, dangerously sexual.

When a woman became aroused by watching a man eat peanut butter and honey, she was in trouble. Big trouble.

He sat back in his chair and drummed his fingers on the arms. "I was hateful and cruel," he said quietly. His voice dropped an octave. "You were trying to express sympathy in the only way you knew how. I acted like a jerk."

She could almost see his frustration. "You were a kid. It was a long time ago. Forget about it."

"Have you?"

The sharp question caught her off guard. "I…uh…no," she muttered. "I never forgot."

After an awkward pause, he handed her some tablets. "These are nonprescription, but Jacob says they'll be the best thing for muscles aches. Take them now so you'll be comfortable in bed."

Their fingers brushed as the medicine changed hands. The word *bed* hovered in the air between them. She clenched her fist. "Thank you."

Without taking his eyes off hers, he covered her hand. "Now," he said hoarsely. "Don't wait. And quit being so damned polite."

She jerked away and swallowed the pills, almost choking because of the knowledge that he had touched her. It meant nothing… She was the one freaking out, not Devlyn. He was merely being a gentleman.

Avoiding his cobralike gaze, she scooped up a shortbread cookie. It melted on her tongue like ambrosia of the gods. "I'd forgotten how good these are," she moaned.

Devlyn reacted visibly to the involuntary sound she made. Feeling her cheeks heat in embarrassment, she bent her head and took another sip of tea. Was it just her, or was Devlyn reacting as strongly as she was to the odd sense of intimacy that shrouded the room in hushed layers?

Three

Devlyn couldn't remember the last time he'd spent this much time in a woman's bedroom without both of them getting naked. When Gillian made a surprisingly sexual response to cookies...goddamned sugar cookies, his sex hardened from zero to sixty in five seconds.

And she wasn't even pretty in the traditional sense.

He adjusted himself unobtrusively and ate another sandwich. Maybe if he kept his mouth full he could quit thinking about licking his way down that swanlike white-skinned neck. Good lord...

"So tell me, Gillian. What do you do for a living...when you're not smashing cars into trees?"

She stared at him with affront.

"Too soon?" He grinned at her, surprisingly entertained by the unexpected turn his evening had taken. The quick phone call to his investor had not been pleasant, but Devlyn was determined. The outlook might be grim, but he'd fought his way out of worse situations.

Gillian wiped her mouth daintily with a snowy cloth napkin, leaving a faint trace of pink color on the fabric. Seeing the stain from her lips, he imagined other oral scenarios. Perhaps because her lips were the only truly curvy thing about her. They belonged more to a porn star than to a quiet, wary-eyed, little mouse.

She curled her legs beneath her, drawing attention to slim thighs and a narrow waist. He wondered if he could span that waist with his two hands.

Gillian seemed blissfully oblivious to his baser instincts. "Do you joke about everything?" she asked, disapproval evident in her wide-set eyes.

He shrugged. "I'd rather laugh than cry."

And there it was again. That pesky, awful memory. *Hell.* He hadn't meant to bring it up again…or had he?

She cocked her head. "Why did I make you so angry that day?" she asked. "I've always wondered. Was it only because I saw you in tears?"

Any humor he'd tried to generate evaporated. He leaped to his feet and stoked the fire, throwing on another couple of logs for good measure. Leaning an arm on the mantel, he poked at the embers, wishing he didn't feel the same prodding at a place that would never heal.

"Sure," he said curtly. "That was it."

"You're lying."

He jerked around so quickly that he knocked over one of the andirons. Replacing it clumsily, he sat down hard in his chair, staring at her with bemused eyes. "I don't know what to make of you, Gillian Carlyle. So let's go back to my first question. What do you do for a living?"

"I'm a teacher. Third grade." Pride glowed on her face and in her voice until something stole it away, some weary acceptance of an unpalatable truth. "Or I was," she said, her tone subdued. "The county I worked for outside of Charlottesville cut forty positions last week. I was four years into a five-year tenure track."

"That sucks."

"Tell me about it."

Their eyes met, and they both burst into laughter. Devlyn realized in that instant that he had been wrong earlier. Gillian Carlyle wasn't plain. She was a beauty. But it was the hidden loveliness of the sea on a cloudy, windswept day. Only when the sun came out were the emeralds and sapphires and aquamarines revealed.

His brain whirred with sudden possibilities. "Is that why you're back home in Burton?"

"Partially. I begged my mother to move to Charlottesville with me when I got the job, but she never would. She loves the house where I grew up, and oddly enough, she loves Wolff Castle. She's very proud to be part of the staff here, and she doesn't want to leave."

"So why did you try to persuade her?"

"My dad was a carpenter. He died a few years ago when scaffolding at a worksite collapsed. Mama was distraught, and I wanted her where I could keep an eye on her. In case you hadn't noticed, there are no teaching jobs around here. Not many jobs of any kind for someone with my training."

"But she wouldn't move."

"No. And now she's glad she didn't. But that still leaves me in a tough spot, because I want to look after her, but I can't even take care of myself at the moment."

"Something will come up." He had an idea or two, but now was not the time. "Would you like another cookie?"

Her lips quirked. "I'm not stupid, Devlyn. I answered your questions. Don't you owe me the same courtesy?"

That amazing, adorably boyish smile flashed briefly. "I'm a stubborn SOB. Don't try to analyze me. What you see is what you get."

Her eyes widened as she caught the deliberately flirtatious innuendo. As he watched, her cheeks turned pink. And about the same time, a little frown line appeared between her brows. "I don't think you're a very nice man," she said slowly.

"Nice guys finish last. Don't you know?" He stood and messed with the fire again, irritated as hell that she put him on edge. She was a nobody. An unemployed elementary schoolteacher. A starchy, prissy, sexually repressed female.

Perhaps if he told himself often enough, he would believe it.

Gillian yawned suddenly, and he felt a lick of remorse. She'd been through a hell of a lot. It was long past time for her to be in bed. But not in his.

He stood up and held out his hand. "C'mon, little lady. You're drooping."

She stood and began stacking their dirty dishes.

"Leave them," he said, a hand on her arm. "The staff will get it in the morning."

Gillian froze, and immediately, he heard how his words must have sounded to her. Heat stained his throat. "I'm sorry," he said gruffly. "That was insensitive."

Gillian shrugged, causing the fabric of her top to mold to her bare, small, perfect breasts. He swallowed hard, caught unawares by a sudden driving urge to unbutton that top and look his fill.

She smiled wryly. "Don't be stupid. Your family provides a lot of great jobs for working-class people. That's not a bad thing."

But she didn't say it was good, either. He sensed her ambivalence and her fatigue. "Go to bed, Gillian. You're beat. We can talk in the morning, but if you need me during the night, don't play the martyr. I'm right next door."

Gillian tossed and turned for an hour, unable to sleep in a strange house. The medicine had taken the edge off her various pains, but her body still ached. At last, she climbed out of bed and went to the French doors, drawing the thick draperies aside and peering out into the dark.

A tiny crescent moon cast a dim light that filtered down like fairy dust among the trees that surrounded the house. When Wolff Castle was built, Devlyn's father and his uncle had been insistent that as little of the woods as possible be cut down. Consequently, the forest cloaked the enormous house like a security blanket, maintaining the privacy for which the Wolffs were famed.

The late-night scene was serene. Gillian's emotions were anything but. She felt trapped, claustrophobic. Even if she had the energy and the will to do so, she couldn't leave. Her car was crumpled at the bottom of the mountain.

Her mother's voice had been hard to read when Gillian called her to explain what had happened. Doreen Carlyle was well acquainted with all the members of the Wolff family, including Devlyn. And Devlyn's reputation with the opposite sex was no secret.

Women loved him. And he loved women. But never for more than a season, at best. Though he seemed like an open book, dark currents ran beneath his easy charm and his outrageous sex appeal.

Gillian curled her fist in a fold of cloth and shivered as her bare toes chilled on the flagstones that edged the doorway. Dare she go outside? Would anyone know?

Without another thought, she pulled her thick sweater over the fancy pajamas and shoved her feet into her boots. Even without a mirror, she knew she looked ludicrous. But she had to escape, had to prove to herself that she wasn't a prisoner. A small, spiral, wrought-iron staircase at the end of her balcony offered easy access to the level below.

The air was colder than she had anticipated. Rain had finally moved on, and indigo skies overhead were clear, allowing the temperature to plummet. Fall would soon give way to winter, especially at this elevation. She followed a pathway at random, not at all worried about being alone in the dark.

She was a country girl, born and raised in these mountains. Travelers came from across the globe to see the mystical and beautiful Blue Ridge, but for Gillian they were more like an old, comfortable friend.

As she meandered, she thought about the last time she had visited Wolff Mountain. She'd been a sophomore in high school, and in her economics class, they'd been doing projects about starting a business. Doreen Carlyle had asked Victor Wolff, Devlyn's uncle, if her daughter could interview him.

Gillian remembered how nervous she had been that day, but Victor Wolff, despite his gruff demeanor, had put her at ease. By the end of the conversation, they had been old buddies. He had a keen intellect and a knack for making money.

As she was leaving the house, preparing to negotiate the long, winding driveway in her fifteen-year-old Volkswagen Beetle, Gillian had come face-to-face with Devlyn Wolff. She remembered how her throat closed up, how hot color flooded her face. Neither of them spoke a word.

Devlyn seemed on the cusp of saying something urgent, but before he could tell her again that she didn't belong, she fled. And until tonight, that was the last time she had ever seen him in the flesh.

The press, however, was another story. Devlyn's exploits both in and out of the boardroom were legendary. He'd bought baseball teams, had at one time even dabbled with driving his own race car. The two Wolff patriarchs had put a quick stop to that, but even so, Devlyn deserved his reputation as a billionaire playboy…an out-of-date term, perhaps, but one that fit.

His wilder party days had tempered as he approached thirty, perhaps because he was being groomed to take over the reins of the family business.

Victor and Vincent Wolff started their families late in life, both of them at least fifteen years older than the beautiful wives they eventually lost.

Now, they were at a point where they wanted to enjoy retirement. So Devlyn was in control of everything. Nothing short of brilliant, he worked as hard as he partied.

Gillian was not immune to his appeal. But he was way out of her league. She preferred bookish, intellectual men, guys who were more like house-trained pets than wild, night-roaming creatures.

Devlyn was incredibly dangerous and yet so very attractive.

She hugged her arms around her body and decided she had had enough. Her limbs trembled with fatigue, and it was time for another dose of painkiller. Things always seemed so much worse at this hour…her bleak employment future, the lack of male companionship in her nunlike life…the hole in her emotions left by her father's passing.

Blinking back tears of self-pity that she refused to let fall, she turned and immediately tripped over a root, stumbling to her knees on the cold and muddy ground.

"What in the hell do you think you're doing?"

Devlyn's outraged voice startled her as much as the fall. In an instant, his hands were under her arms, lifting her effortlessly to her feet. Seeing the state she was in, he cursed beneath his breath and shrugged out of the thick, fleece-lined jacket he wore. He wrapped it around her and scooped her into his arms.

"You can't spend all your time carrying me around," she muttered. But it was a token protest at best. His warmth surrounded her even as his strength filled her with an odd contentment.

It was a false sense of security. She knew that. But for this one moment, this single, unlikely and unsettling reunion, she decided to pretend that she had a right to be here in Devlyn Wolff's embrace.

She had left the double, glass-paned doors to her room un-latched. After negotiating the narrow stairs, Devlyn depos-ited her on her feet long enough to remove her muddy boots and his shoes, before urging her inside, locking the doors and drawing the drapes.

Gillian had left a single lamp burning. The confusion in Devlyn's eyes mirrored her own. "I'm sorry I disturbed you," she said, the words stiff. "I couldn't sleep."

"Same here." Still he stared at her. "Sit down on the bed, Gillian."

He stepped past her, and moments later she heard water running in the bathroom. When he returned, he had a damp washcloth in his hands. "I said sit down."

She sat.

Why was she enabling his bossiness? She was a mature woman with a life that clicked along quite well. She didn't need a man to take care of her.

He took her fingers in his and gently wiped away the mud where she had landed, hands down. His touch was gentle but firm, removing the bits of leaves and grass that clung to her skin.

Next he removed his coat, the one he had wrapped around her. His eyes went to the muddy knees of her pajamas, and her stomach clenched. Surely he wouldn't—

"Lift your hips."

Like an automaton, she obeyed, watching the tableau un-fold as he bared her legs and dragged the pants down to her ankles and away. "Get under the covers," he said.

Her face flaming with color, she obeyed, painfully con-scious that he didn't even bother to avert his gaze. When she was covered from the waist down, she removed the sweater, managing to tangle her hair in the process. Devlyn disappeared into the bathroom a second time and came back holding a brush still wrapped in cellophane.

He sat down beside her, opening the package. "Turn away from me," he commanded.

She felt one hand settle on her shoulder. With the other, he dragged the brush through her hair. Her eyes closed and a whimper of delight escaped her lips. Her head lolled on her shoulders as the simple pleasure unfolded. Occasionally, as he encountered a knot, she felt his fingers sift through her straight, thick tresses.

Gooseflesh erupted all over her body, and her breasts grew heavy with arousal. Did he try this on all his women? God, the man was a genius. He never seemed to tire. The gentle pull of the bristles against her scalp went on and on. Sleepiness gradually replaced sexual excitement.

Dimly, she heard him speak soft words as he eased her onto her back. She felt hard, warm arms encircle her.

After that…nothing.

Four

Devlyn awoke abruptly, his internal alarm clock set for 6:00 a.m. For a moment, he was completely disoriented. And then everything came flooding back. Gillian Carlyle.

Though it was an anomaly to begin the day fully dressed in a woman's bed, the details were clear. He'd been driven by a combination of guilt and lust, determined to take care of the prickly woman who was a thorn in the side of his past.

He rubbed his gritty eyes, wishing he had the option of going back to sleep. But Wolff Enterprises expected him at the helm this morning, and he had already made one costly mistake because of this woman.

Gillian sighed in her sleep and nestled more closely into his embrace. He was on top of the comforter, hard and ready to take her. All she was wearing was a pajama top, and below the covers a next-to-nothing pair of panties. Unable to help himself, he slid a hand beneath the sheet and caressed her bottom.

Gillian sighed and turned to curl an arm around his neck.

Now her breasts were pressed snugly against his arm. He slid his fingers beneath the silk at her hip and felt her warm skin. His body throbbed with arousal. A few more inches and he would be touching her most intimate secrets.

Somewhere in the house he heard muffled laughter. The sound snatched him back to sanity. God in heaven. What was he doing? Had he learned nothing from the past?

He slid from the bed with all the care of a cat burglar hoping to elude detection. It took everything he had to turn his back on Gillian and return to his room. As he showered and dressed, he reminded himself of all the reasons he couldn't start something with his overnight visitor.

First and foremost was Gillian's clear discomfort about the fact that her mother worked for Devlyn's father. Devlyn could not care less, but even so, he acknowledged the difficulty of coaxing Gillian into his bed with little or no privacy for their fledgling relationship, especially when either or both of their parents might not approve.

Secondly, he owed Gillian more than a verbal apology for his shameful actions in the past. Acknowledging that he had been merely a boy when it happened was not enough. He was determined to clean the slate, and he knew just how to do it. He told himself that in this instance he was doing the right thing and not merely perpetuating his tendency to play hero to every woman who crossed his path needing help.

In college, he had supported his roommate's pregnant girlfriend, both emotionally and financially, when the father of her baby dumped her. That altruistic action on Devlyn's part had severed his relationship with a young man he had considered his best friend.

Not only that, the girl had latched on to the idea that lovers were interchangeable…and she set her sights on Devlyn. Only by graduating and moving hundreds of miles away had he been able to extract himself from the messy situation.

Unfortunately, it was a pattern that repeated itself in sub-sequent years. Every time he rushed in on his white horse to save the day, he got screwed. The secretary at work whose brother needed a job ended up hating Devlyn when he finally had to fire her worthless sibling.

Even worse was the fifty-something caterer who had ac-cused Devlyn, over two decades her junior, of sexual harass-ment. He had offered to help her load her van after a staff Christmas party, and the woman had seen a chance to make a quick buck.

The Wolff lawyers settled out of court, costing the fam-ily an indecent amount of money. Now that Devlyn thought about it, it was a miracle that his dad and uncle had trusted him enough to make him CEO.

But despite his sometimes unfortunate judgment in dealing with the female sex, he was a whiz kid when it came to money matters. He'd earned his own first million, aside from the family business, by investments he'd made in his late teens.

The intensity and daily challenge of running the far-flung Wolff empire suited him perfectly. He was due back at his headquarters in Atlanta soon. Barely enough time to pres-ent his proposition to Gillian and ensure that he had finally made amends for the past.

So why was he obsessing over the image of long, slender legs and a sweetly curved bottom? The answer was simple. Logical or not, he wanted her, though she certainly deserved better than the flawed man he was.

Picking up his smartphone from the bureau, he took a deep breath and strode out into the hall. He had a dozen balls to juggle today, and he was already running behind. His per-sonal life could wait.

Gillian rolled over and glanced at the clock, her muddled brain trying to understand why both hands pointed straight up toward the twelve. Then everything came rushing back. Her accident, the multiple disturbing and faintly erotic encounters with Devlyn Wolff. Her lack of a job.

Not the best memories with which to begin a day in which her body felt like an old woman's. She turned her head carefully, hoping to stave off the jackhammers that threatened to crush her skull. Though she was alone in the bed, the pillow beside her bore the unmistakable imprint of someone's head. When she tugged it closer for a sniff, the soft, expensive fabric emanated the unmistakable scent of Devlyn Wolff.

Holy cow. What had she done? Squeezing her eyes shut, she reached for images that hid in random corners of her brain. She remembered going outside. She even remembered Devlyn bringing her in and watching her take off her pants. At that point, things became hazy.

He had touched her hair…had lulled her to sleep. Then what? Surely the memory of his big, warm hand on her butt was a dream.

Stumbling into the bathroom, she splashed water on her face and noted in surprise the neatly folded pile of clean clothes that turned out to be a khaki skirt and a black scooped-neck T-shirt with a matching thin cardigan.

The clothes fit perfectly, which in itself was alarming. A man who could choose women's apparel with such an eye was a man with far too much experience in pleasing women.

Her boots were still muddy, perhaps beyond repair, but her stealthy benefactor had included a pair of black canvas espadrilles. The shoes were a little too large, but she stuffed tissues in the toes until she was certain they were snug enough to stay on her feet.

Feeling a bit too much like Little Orphan Annie, she finally opened the envelope that lay like a coiled serpent on the bedside table.

Please join me for lunch in the library at one. Devlyn.

The house was still and quiet, almost somnolent, as if everyone in the *Sleeping Beauty* castle snoozed for a thousand years. Thank God her mother was not scheduled to work today. Gillian's face would have given her away, her mother seeing at once that her daughter had fallen under the spell of a Wolff prince.

Gillian remembered the way to the library with ease. It was another place where Doreen Carlyle had kept her daughter entertained while she worked. Gillian had always been a compliant child, not one to make messes or break things. She had been more than content to curl up on the velvet-covered bench seat in the window alcove and read her favorite books for hours at a time.

In many ways, the Wolff Castle library had been her magic carpet, taking her to lands beyond the horizon, introducing her to characters whose lives were far more exotic than her own. The library had been her haven, her cozy nest. When she was there, she felt safe.

But nothing about today's visit inspired such warm, fuzzy feelings. When she opened the door, Devlyn was already in residence, his stance at the fireplace much like the night before in her bedroom. His lips curved in a welcoming smile, but his eyes were watchful.

"Good afternoon, Gillian. I hope you were finally able to get some sleep."

He was playing with her, trying to make her nervous. She knew beyond a shadow of a doubt that he had been the one to enter her room and drop off the clothes and the note.

"Yes," she said stiffly. "I did. I need to check on my car."

He shrugged. "Already taken care of…. The garage will drop it off at your mother's house by the end of the week."

She bit her bottom lip. "I'd like an estimate. So I can contact my insurance."

"Let me handle this. It's the least I can do. You know they'll jack up your rates if you submit it."

He had her there. And she couldn't afford the current payments, much less a rate hike. "I'll pay you back."

His brows narrowed in displeasure. "I said to forget it."

"You like ruling the world, don't you? Is there anyone who says no to you?"

Her sass seemed to amuse him. "Sit down, Gillian. Chef has prepared an autumn vegetable chowder that I'm told is to die for."

She joined him at the table, wondering what his family thought of his absence from the communal dining room. Of course, with Jacob out of town and the others perhaps tucked away in their own houses, maybe Victor and Vincent dined alone.

Devlyn picked up his spoon and dug in, polishing off his bowl of soup and three rolls before Gillian had barely started. It was hard to swallow anything past the constriction in her throat, even though Devlyn was correct about the delicious, hearty broth. Finally, the silence weighed too heavily for her to finish. She pushed back from the table and folded her hands in her lap.

The fire was warm—warm enough for her to discard her sweater. But she fancied she needed the extra layer of protection. "You left me a note," she said bluntly. "Why am I here?"

"I could have guessed you were a teacher, even if you hadn't told me."

The odd segue baffled her. "What does that mean?"

"You're uptight, bossy, no-nonsense…"

"And you've deduced all that in a mere twenty-four hours?"

"Less than that. I expect any moment to get my knuckles rapped with a ruler."

His air of masculine superiority set her teeth on edge. "That's an archaic reference."

"You don't know the tutors my father and uncle hired."

"Poor little rich boy." She regretted the words immediately. In many ways, the appellation was true...or at least had been in the past. Devlyn Wolff as a child and a teen had always seemed angry. And with good reason. He'd lost his mother violently. Been snatched away from the only home he had ever known and brought to this isolated mountain. Had not been allowed to attend school where he would have made friends. It was no wonder the six cousins were so close.

She didn't know how to characterize him now...that would require spending time together, a notion that alarmed and intrigued her at the same time. "We're getting off topic," she said, her voice firm...the one she used for recalcitrant boys on the playground. "What do you want to talk to me about?"

"I want to hire you."

Her hackles went up. "You apologized. I accepted. I don't need your charity simply because I'm unemployed."

"Before you ride that high horse off into the sunset, why don't you listen for a minute? I need to employ a teacher. It might as well be you."

Her stomach cramped. Did Devlyn have a child she hadn't heard about? "There are no schools anywhere near Wolff Mountain."

He grinned as if he had scored a hit. "My point exactly. Evidently you haven't heard, but the Wolffs are establishing a school in Burton."

"Thumbing your nose at the locals? No one around here can afford private tuition."

"Gillian, Gillian..." He shook his head. "I'm talking about a public school. And that's why I need you. It's a sticky proposition to make sure all of the accreditation requirements are fulfilled. And we've had a hell of a time convincing the administration that we'll stay out of the day-to-day running. But this is going to happen. The children of Burton have every right to attend school in their own community."

Gillian was stunned. What he said made perfect sense, but although the Wolffs were active in a number of charities, this project took benevolence to another whole level. "Whose idea was this?"

"It was a family decision. Too many of our staff worry that if one of their children gets sick, or falls on the playground, it would be a good forty-five minutes before they could get to the school. That's not acceptable. The economy is in the toilet. Money for new schools is scarce. We have the means to supply a need."

Gillian cocked her head, studying his face. He seemed genuinely excited and proud. "And you're spearheading the effort?"

"Mostly. Because I'm the one in charge. But all of us will step in at various points. Kieran's wife is a children's illustrator. She's planning to paint murals on all the walls. Jacob will design and outfit a small in-school clinic and hire a nurse. Gareth wants to build custom shelving for the library. I could go on…"

She held up a hand, feeling ashamed of her suspicions. On occasion, that chip on her shoulder about the rich gained weight again. "It's a lovely idea. I'm impressed. But I still don't see where I come in. It will be a long time until you're ready to hire teachers."

"I need a liaison…someone who will work side by side with me, but who knows how to communicate with state and local officials."

"But you work out of Atlanta."

"I'm here at least one weekend a month, sometimes two. Dad and Uncle Vic like to feel as if they are still part of the decision-making process. And I value their experience. But in regard to this school project, you'll be my point person. We'll work very closely together."

"I don't know what to say."

"Say you'll do it."

He named a salary that was over twice what she was making before the layoffs. Only a fool would turn down this opportunity, but then again, working with Devlyn Wolff would not be easy. He was charming and outrageously handsome and had a wicked sense of humor…all qualities that were destined to make a woman like Gillian fall into infatuation at the very least.

And she was pretty sure she wasn't imagining the sexual vibe between them. What was alarming was that if she succumbed, not only did she endanger yet another good job, but she risked getting her heart broken. "Who would you have hired if I hadn't come along?" It was hard to put her suspicions to rest.

"I hadn't gotten that far yet, but I called your principal this morning, and she speaks very highly of you…told me you were named 'Teacher of the Year' in your school last year. She's really upset about losing you."

"You investigated me?" The words ended on a screech of outrage.

"Your ID badge was sticking out of the side pocket of your purse. I'm a businessman. And despite your weird hang-ups, I'm not offering you this job because of something that happened when we were kids."

He could deny it all he wanted, but she was almost a hundred percent sure that Devlyn was the kind of man who needed to even the scales. This was his way of assuaging his guilt over the past.

Still, who was she to turn down a boon because of his

screwed-up motives? She needed a job. And this would be a good one.

"I'll do it," she said. "When do I start?"

Five

Devlyn high-fived his inner self, but managed to maintain a neutral expression. This was exactly the same feeling he got when he outwitted a difficult opponent in a business deal. He didn't probe too deeply at why it was so important to win over Gillian, but it was.

"You'll need to move in here," he said abruptly, thinking on his feet. The idea of having Gillian just down the hall made his pulse thud with anticipation.

She scowled, standing up and pacing with her arms wrapped around her waist. "That won't be necessary. The commute is not inconvenient."

"It's not your convenience we're talking about…it's mine. I'm a very busy man. When I can snatch a few minutes to discuss the school project, I'd like for you to be available."

Gillian's spine straightened and her chin lifted. "So in essence, you're hiring me to be at your beck and call."

He wanted to chuckle aloud. She was pissed. And it was

so much damned fun aggravating her. "Think of it more as a lawyer on retainer."

Her eyes shot daggers at him. Fuming, frustrated, she seemed about to burst with aggravation. "I'm not sure I trust you."

"You wound me." He put his hand over his heart. "What exactly do you think I have up my sleeve?"

"I don't know you well enough to tell."

"I'd like to get to know *you,* Gillian." He hadn't meant to say that. The words tumbled out uncensored, but they were true. Something about her seemed so real, so honest. In his experience, those were qualities rarely found in female companionship. Gillian knew as much or more about him, warts and all, than most people did. And he had an inexplicable urge to win her approval.

But the devil in him couldn't leave it alone. "I'll have a driver out front in fifteen minutes to take you to your mother's house so you can pack your things. I'd like you to be back on the mountain by five. I want to take you to see the property we've purchased…get your impressions."

She sat back down abruptly and started eating soup. "I'm not finished with my lunch. Better make it forty-five." She gave him a bland gaze that did little to disguise her intent. It was clear that she wouldn't be pushed around.

The businessman in him applauded her chutzpah. The hungry male took it as a challenge. This give-and-take was foreplay whether she realized it or not. The circumstances weren't ideal. He'd already made a list of "cons." But if Gillian felt the same sexual pull he did, he'd figure a way around the difficulties. He wasn't accustomed to denying himself when it came to women. Nothing permanent could come of this. He was not the pure, uncomplicated man Gillian needed for the long haul.

Devlyn Wolff, however, did *temporary* damned well. Gillian might try to hide her sexuality beneath generic clothing, but he could see the possibilities. And they excited him.

"Remember," he said, "You're agreeing to be here 24/7 anytime I'm in town. I want to get my money's worth."

Those big, beautiful eyes reflected shock and denial. "But you're not home all that often."

"At the moment, that's true. So we'll have to rely on emails and late night phone calls, won't we?"

"Late night?" Her voice squeaked.

"Some days that's the only time I can break free. Do you have a problem with that?"

She shredded a roll between her long, graceful fingers. "I don't suppose so. But I'm not sure what my mother will think about all of this."

"You've been on your own a long time, right?"

"Yes."

"Then what's the problem?"

She pursed her lips as if she had bitten into a sour spice. "You have quite a reputation in regard to the opposite sex."

"But ours is a business relationship. I'm sure your mother understands the difference."

"I guess…" Her hesitance aroused him as he imagined what it would take to coax her into his bed. In the past six months his schedule had been brutal. Workaholic was an understatement.

Life was too short not to play when the occasion presented itself. And Gillian Carlyle, as reserved and wary as she was, promised to be endlessly entertaining.

He glanced at his watch. "I'm afraid I can't drag this out any longer. I'm overdue for several phone calls. But I'll expect you back here at five…right?"

She nodded her head slowly. "I'll be here. You can count on it."

Devlyn forced himself to leave the room. If he pushed too

hard, she might decide to walk out, unemployed or not. And he couldn't have that.

He found his father, Vincent, and his Uncle Vic in Victor's study. Pipe smoke hung heavy in the air, and a chessboard sat between their armchairs, resting on a marble-topped table.

His father looked up when he entered. "Don't distract us. This is a hell of a game."

Devlyn took up residence on a sofa adjacent to the fireplace and pulled out his phone to begin working through emails. Soon he was immersed in the day-to-day operation of a global, multibillion dollar company. Some days it baffled him to realize the enormous enterprise he steered on behalf of the family. The responsibility was huge. But damned if he didn't love it.

Finally, the game wound to an end. Uncle Vic stood up and stretched. "I'm not too proud to say I need a nap. Didn't sleep worth crap last night. It's a sad day when a man can't drink coffee at midnight anymore."

Devlyn grinned. The two brothers were peas in a pod, always much alike in outlook, but bound together eternally by the horrific experiences of their young wives' deaths.

Neither had ever considered remarriage as far as Devlyn could tell. They had devoted themselves to rearing their combined six children far away from the limelight. It was a testament to their love and generosity that several of those children had returned to make Wolff Mountain their home.

Devlyn couldn't imagine staying here permanently, but at the moment, he was prepared to make some temporary changes. After his dad refilled his pipe and gave a few puffs that sent aromatic scent into the air, the old man perched on the other end of the divan.

His skin was leathery from years spent in the sun, but his dark eyes were as shrewd and sharp as ever. "What's on your mind, Devvie?"

The childish nickname didn't bother Devlyn. He knew his father respected him as an adult. He grinned. "What would you think if I set up a more permanent office here…for the next six months?"

His dad snorted. "You're up to something. I've seen that look a million times…starting with the first time you took off your diaper and smeared poo on the walls."

Devlyn winced. "For God's sakes, old man. Can we please not share that story? I'm almost thirty-one years old. It's embarrassing."

Vincent shrugged. "You'll always be my kid. Which is why I know you're plotting something. Details, boy. Give this old geezer a treat."

Devlyn's smile was wry. His father had the body of a much younger man. He ate an extremely healthy diet, despite the cigars. He was likely to live for another twenty years.

Devlyn grinned. "I just hired Gillian Carlyle to help us with the school project."

"The housekeeper's daughter?"

For some reason, the tops of Devlyn's ears got hot. "She's a fully certified teacher…comes highly recommended."

"Then why is she free right now?"

"Layoffs. Not her fault."

"Hmph."

"What?" He hadn't anticipated any guff about his decision.

"Are you thinking with your brain or your—"

"Hell, Dad." Devlyn cut him off quickly. "Give me some credit."

"I've seen the woman. She may be a tad more restrained in her clothing choices than your usual women, but there's a quiet beauty about her."

It was a little weird to hear his father say aloud what Devlyn had been thinking. "I'm hiring her for her expertise, not her suitability as a girlfriend."

"Then why move in here?"

Well, crap. The old man hasn't lost it.

"Okay," Devlyn admitted. "I don't hate the idea of getting to know her better. She's a quirky little thing. But we really do need her help. And we know she's not going to steal the silver or sell us out to the tabloids."

The Wolffs had endured their share of sensational gossip-rag stories. And outsiders were always an unknown quantity. Which made Gillian appealing in another way entirely. She was one of them in a sense.

His father stared a hole through him. "Who'll be minding the store in Atlanta?"

"A new kid. Well, new to management. I've been watching him. He's brilliant and driven. He lives for the job. I thought this would be a good opportunity to see what he can do."

"Okay, then. You have my blessing. And you know I'll enjoy having that ugly face of yours around." Vincent Wolff got to his feet. Devlyn rose out of respect and the two of them embraced briefly. It was awkward. Only in recent years had his dad been able to openly express paternal affection.

The past held too many ghosts, too many secrets. But Devlyn was all about the future.

Gillian was happy to find her mother home when she made the trip back down the mountain. The little one-level house where Gillian had grown up was as different from Wolff Castle as bologna from prime rib. But though genteelly shabby and quietly dated, it was home.

Doreen Carlyle embraced her daughter, smelling of Jergens lotion and fresh air. "Aunt Tina says hello. She wants you to go down for a visit while you have some flexibility."

"Welcome home." Gillian hovered as her mother put away three bags of groceries. For several years after Gillian's father died, Doreen had been a wraith, unable to imagine a world without her high-school sweetheart. But gradually she had returned to the world of the living, and Gillian would be forever grateful for her mother's resiliency.

Doreen hummed as she worked, a habit that used to annoy her daughter as a teenager, but now seemed like the most natural thing in the world. Gillian perched on a stool at the counter. "Have you heard anything about the Wolffs building a school here in Burton?"

Her mother paused momentarily, her back to Gillian, and then turned around, with a sheepish expression. "I heard about it for the first time last week, but I didn't want you to get your hopes up. It will be a long time until they are ready to start hiring teachers, honey."

"Devlyn Wolff offered me a job today."

Doreen sat down in a chair, a bag of sugar still clutched in her hands. "How in the world did that happen?"

"It's a long story. We ran into each other last night...I mentioned that I was out of work, and he offered me the job."

Doreen had a keen *mother* radar. "Gillian Elizabeth Carlyle. What have you done?"

"Nothing, Mama. I thought you'd be happy for me."

"Those Wolffs are my bread-and-butter, but I wasn't born yesterday. Devlyn Wolff is a rascal. And a skirt chaser."

"That's not fair. He can't help it if women pursue him because he's rich and gorgeous." Gillian found herself in the strange position of defending the man she had sworn to hold at arm's length.

"So you think he's gorgeous."

Gillian felt her cheeks flush. "I think everybody would agree on that."

"Hmm..." Her mother's assessing gaze appeared to see right through to Gillian's inherent ambivalence. It was thrilling to have a job. And Devlyn Wolff would be a fascinating boss. But the road ahead was booby-trapped with a thousand potential heartbreaks.

"There's one other thing…" She might as well get it over with.

"What?" Doreen's eyebrows rose, projecting alarm.

"He wants me to stay at the castle now and then…when he's there. So I'll be on hand when he has time to deal with the school project."

"Gillian, Gillian, Gillian." Doreen shook her head. "Do you remember that guy who gave you an engagement ring your sophomore year in college?"

"Yes, ma'am."

"I tried to warn you that he was using you."

"And I wouldn't listen." The boy had been far more interested in having Gillian cook for him and do his laundry than anything else. The engagement had lasted a mere four months.

"You're a grown woman now, entirely capable of making your own mistakes. But you're still my baby, and I still worry about you."

Doreen didn't mention the other debacle, and Gillian was grateful. In her first teaching job, the male principal had shown a marked interest in what Gillian thought was *mentoring* her. Unfortunately, the man had a reputation for inappropriate conduct with fresh-out-of-school young women. That situation had ended up with a sexual harassment lawsuit involving half a dozen new teachers.

Gillian had moved on to another school, but she had lost confidence in her ability to spot liars and con men. She didn't really think Devlyn Wolff fell into either category. But he was dangerous in an entirely different way. Devlyn's charm and knee-melting masculinity had the potential to make a female not care that he was leading her down the garden path.

A stint in Devlyn's bed, no matter how brief, might ruin

a woman for other men. That alone should be the cautionary tale to keep Gillian from doing something stupid.

She needed a job. Devlyn was prepared to pay her well for her expertise as an educator. Even if he flirted with her— and it seemed to be an inescapable facet of his personality— there was no way Gillian would allow herself to get sucked into believing that she was any more to him than a convenient warm body.

Surely she had learned her lesson. And Devlyn was an honorable man. He wouldn't pull anything sleazy…she knew that. The real danger was Gillian herself. All else aside, she had to remember that despite political correctness, princes didn't form lasting relationships with scullery maids, at least not in real life.

Gillian needed to meet a man who wanted what she wanted. Home, family, ordinary happiness. If she kept that in mind, all would be well.

Six

Devlyn found himself pacing the foyer at a quarter till five. What if she didn't come? He had rescheduled a late dinner with his investor from the night before, but in the meantime he had just enough of a window to take Gillian to see the land for the school.

The fact that he was anticipating her arrival with such emotion brought him up short. He knew himself fairly well, knew his tendencies to coddle women, to look after them. He'd been doing it with his sister, Annalise, since she was an infant in the cradle. Devlyn had been her protector, her white knight.

But he and his sibling had clashed during her late teenage years. Annalise was headstrong, and at that point in her life didn't take kindly to her brother interfering. Fortunately the two of them had mended fences a long time ago. His sister was one of his best friends.

With other women in his life—at least the ones he was attracted to—he'd never been able to maintain a platonic relationship. He was pretty sure he didn't want Gillian to be the first test case.

The front door opened abruptly, and Gillian burst through. Her expression was not exactly sweetness and light. *Grumpy* might be the word for it.

She set her overnight case on the floor. "Why am I here when you could have picked me up at my house and saved me a trip up the mountain?"

He grinned. "We're going to do an aerial reconnaissance first."

Her face went green. "Um, no. I don't do flying things."

"Come on, Gillian. It will be fun, I swear. And besides, you don't want me to dock your first paycheck already. You're on the clock…remember?"

"I think I may possibly hate you." Her glare might have intimidated another man. Devlyn took it as a challenge.

He laughed out loud, putting a hand beneath her elbow and escorting her out a side door and through the woods up to the helipad. "Climb in," he said cheerfully. Everyone was timid about being in a helicopter at first. But give her a few minutes airborne, seeing the verdant Virginia countryside from an eagle's eye view, and she'd be entranced.

Ten minutes into the flight Gillian had her head inside a barf bag. Losing her lunch…literally. The pitiful moan that reached Devlyn's ears made his stomach curl with guilt. How was he supposed to know she was serious? Did the woman never travel?

He stroked her hair tentatively, wincing every time she retched. "How about some water…that might help."

She shoved his hand away and threw up again.

Devlyn ripped off his headset and scuttled forward to crouch beside the pilot. "Land the damn chopper. Now."

The man looked at him incredulously. They were skimming over a thick forest. "It will be a few minutes."

"As quickly as you can." In the back of his mind lurked the knowledge that he was going to miss another shot at his investor. But circumstances were beyond his control.

Devlyn strapped himself back into his seat and rubbed Gillian's hair. He'd made some dumb-ass mistakes in his life, but this was near the top of his list. Was he destined to make Gillian Carlyle miserable?

After what seemed like hours, but must have been only five minutes or so, the helicopter floated to the ground, landing with a gentle thump in an overgrown field.

The chopper pilot gazed at Devlyn inquiringly. "You want me to wait until she feels better?"

Devlyn glanced at Gillian, who was huddled in her seat, eyes closed, face paper-white. "Not gonna happen. Head back to the castle. Tell them where we are. Send a car for us and a second driver to take both of them back."

While Devlyn helped Gillian out onto steady ground, the pilot gathered up a container of snacks and drinks, a thick canvas tarp lined on one side with reflective material and a another thinner, softer blanket. He stared at Devlyn in confusion. "We traveled as the crow flies, but it's going to be a half hour at least before someone drives here from the castle. Are you sure she'll be okay?"

Devlyn, his eyes on Gillian's wobbly stance, shrugged. "Don't have much choice. I'm not putting her back in that chopper. Hurry, man. As fast as you can."

After waiting for Devlyn and Gillian to move away to a safe distance, the pilot revved up the engine and lifted skyward. The wind wash from the rotors sent Gillian's hair flying in a halo around her head.

Silence fell, and Devlyn spread the tarp rapidly. "Sit down," he commanded. "You look like you're going faint."

"I need my purse," she said, her voice little more than a thread.

He stared down at the giant, black leather tote the pilot had left behind along with the few supplies. "What for?"

"Toothpaste." She swayed, going at least two shades whiter.

He grabbed her just as her knees gave out. "Easy. I've got you."

She curled into a fetal position, and he covered her with the thin fleece blanket. Her arm outstretched, she pointed. "I've got toothpaste in there."

With a sigh for her stubbornness, he rummaged in her things until he located a travel-size toothbrush and toothpaste. She also had hand wipes, baby lotion, tampons, two maps and an assortment of other odd *necessities*.

"Here," he said, holding out what she had asked for.

"Water bottle."

He watched, incredulous, as she scuttled to the edge of the tarp, opened the bottle and proceeded to brush her teeth, spitting into the grass. "I would have thought about kissing you anyway," he said, sitting back on his haunches until she finished.

That made her head whip up, her gaze wary as she wiped her mouth. "Don't be ridiculous. I could sue your family for sexual harassment and drag the Wolff reputation through the dirt." A raw throat made her voice husky.

"But you wouldn't. I know that and you know that. Come here, little schoolmarm. Let me hold you."

It was a testament to her misery that she didn't fight him. The sun was getting low, and the October day was cool and windy. They lay side by side on the tarp. Devlyn spooned her, tucking the blanket over and around them, his arm around her waist.

Gillian's fuzzy lavender sweater and gauzy print skirt in matching shades suited her. Her mostly straight hair tumbled across her face. He nuzzled her cheek with his. "I'm sorry," he said. "I'm going to listen to you from now on."

Her muffled laugh indicated disbelief. He drew her closer. "It's true. I shouldn't have bullied you."

"Why did you hire me?" she asked, the words almost inaudible. "The truth, please."

Where her bottom nestled against the cradle of his thighs, he was hard, aching. Every time he got close to her, his body went on high alert. It was disconcerting as hell. And inexplicable.

"I need an education professional to oversee details that are not my area of expertise."

"And you felt guilty because you were mean to me as a child and I was unemployed."

He stirred uneasily. "Okay…maybe. But that wasn't the primary reason."

"And you've been flirting with me. Explain that."

He concentrated on the pain from a rock that lay somewhere beneath his hip. "I like you," he said, unwilling or unable to expand upon that theme.

"Do you hit on every woman you meet?"

"Only the ones I want to take to bed."

She rolled onto her back without warning, shaded her eyes with one hand and stared at him. "Why me?"

"Why not?"

"That's not an answer."

"I don't have an answer," he growled, wondering why in the hell women had this insatiable need to pick everything apart. "Are you feeling any better?" Perhaps if he distracted her, she would change the subject.

"As long as you don't make me stand up anytime soon, I might live."

"There are lots of things we could do lying down."

"You are such a guy."

"Is that an actual complaint?" He touched her belly, just beneath the swell of her breasts. "I like you, Gillian Carlyle."

Her teeth mutilated her bottom lip. "No offense, but you're not really my type."

"And what is your type?" The scent of her shampoo was making him hungry. They were lying in the middle of some farmer's field, and all he could think about was lifting that fluffy, frilly skirt and taking her wildly.

"I want to get married."

Five simple words blunted his ardor.

"And I want to have children."

He removed his hand. "Is the biological clock that loud?"

She scooted to her side, leaned on an elbow and propped her head on her hand. Now they were facing each other. "It's a fairly normal goal for a woman my age. And you are clearly not a candidate for domestic bliss."

"What's wrong with a little recreational sex in the meantime?"

"You're like a hot fudge sundae," she said, a tiny frown creasing her brow. "They're a great treat on occasion, but if you're going to eat ice cream every day, vanilla is a much better choice. It's easy to get burned out on hot fudge."

"I'm sure such convoluted reasoning makes sense to you, but now all I can think about is licking chocolate sauce off your—"

She put a hand over his mouth. "Behave. You don't really want to do this."

"Oh, but I do." He licked her fingers, and her little *oh* of surprise hit him straight in the gut.

Instead of moving away, she stared at him. And he could swear that somewhere in those deep brown eyes lurked a snippet of interest.

She sighed. "Have you ever had a single serious relationship in your life?"

Perhaps she expected him to lie, but something about Gillian Carlyle made him want to be a better man. Starting with honesty. "No. Not really. And you?"

"A couple of false starts. But at least I believe in the concept."

"You're talking about love."

"Yes. And commitment."

"I'm not domesticated," he said. "I don't need dirty diapers and 3:00 a.m. feedings to be happy."

"But sex can make you happy?"

"I like to live in the moment. The future holds no guarantees. So, yes…on occasion, sex makes me happy."

He had her there. Saw it in her face. He reached out a hand and caressed her cheek.

"I've known you for years, Gillian. But I don't really *know* you. I'd like to change that."

"Why are you doing this?"

He'd never had a woman question his motives so deeply. "I'm not really sure. I've learned to rely on my instincts, though. They've served me well in business."

"And in your personal life?"

He shrugged. "I've made a misstep here and there. But don't we all when it comes to sex?"

"Not all of us take the smorgasbord approach. I've been with two men in my life, Devlyn. Can you even count yours with both hands and feet?"

"I don't sleep with men."

"Don't be a smart-ass. You know what I mean."

He should be angry. No other person of his acquaintance, male or female, would have the balls to cross-examine him about his sex life. But somehow he felt obligated to give Gillian the unvarnished truth. "It's complicated."

"I'm a smart woman."

Her steady gaze studied him and found him wanting. He rolled to his back and tucked his hands behind his head. The

October sky was so blue, it seemed unreal. At the far edge of the field a row of sugar maples flamed, red and orange, against an azure backdrop.

"You know that my father and my uncle didn't allow any of us to go to school."

"Yes."

"We were scarcely allowed off the property…and then only with bodyguards. For a horny teenage guy, it was hell. I dreamed about girls all the time."

"It must have been a strange sort of adolescence."

He laughed without amusement. "You could say that. The only way we were allowed to go away to college was if we used assumed names and swore never to tell a soul who we really were."

"I imagine that created a lot of difficult situations."

"Yeah. Ask Kieran sometime what it did to him. But anyway, I had decided that as soon as I got on campus I was going to screw the first girl who gave me a chance."

"And did you?"

His throat tight, he debated what he was about to say. No one knew this, not even his brother and sister. He couldn't look at Gillian, so he stared up at the sky.

Finally, he stumbled over the first few words. "The summer before I left home, my dad and Uncle Vic hired a husband/wife team to update the landscaping at the castle. The new employees were both in their early thirties, a young couple trying to run their own business and make a living. The woman was beautiful. And since she was working outside in the heat, she wore little shorts and halter tops…"

He swallowed, still able to see her even now. "I was obsessed with watching her. One day I was up in my bedroom with the window open. I heard the two of them arguing. And I saw him backhand her so hard she fell to her knees."

"Oh, Devlyn…"

"I flew down the stairs, ran outside, but he had disappeared. I really believe that if he had still been there I would have beaten him up. Hitting a woman... God, even I, green as I was, knew it was wrong."

"What did you do?"

"She was crying, almost hysterical. I tried to talk to her, but she was embarrassed. There was a big red mark on her cheek, and she didn't want anyone to see. I suggested taking a walk in the woods so she could calm down."

"And she agreed?"

"Yes. We were gone for a long time. I showed her the cave. I was so proud to be able to help her. I could tell that she was happy I was with her. We sat down near the entrance, you know, just cross-legged in the dirt. She told me that she was going to divorce him...that it wasn't the first time he had hit her. But she was worried about money. I don't know what made me do it, but I put my arm around her and told her that I would help her."

He felt Gillian's hand on his shoulder. "You don't have to tell me this," she whispered.

It was too late to stop now. Reliving it all made his stomach hurt. "I know I was naive, but I told her I had money of my own. In my room. That it wouldn't be a loan. She could have it, no questions asked."

"What did she say?"

"She started crying again. And then she kissed me."

Seven

Shock and distress left Gillian almost speechless. She was pretty sure she knew where this story was heading, and her heart bled for Devlyn.

He kept talking, almost as if he had forgotten she was beside him. "I didn't know what to do. It was weird and awkward and wonderful all at the same time. But she was married. And I knew that."

"She took advantage of you, Devlyn."

"Who's to say? I didn't waste much time weighing right and wrong. We undressed and then we…well, you know."

He fell silent. Gillian felt somehow as if the world had shifted on its axis. She didn't know Devlyn at all, not really. Except to understand that he had a streak of caring that ran soul deep when it came to women. He was a protector, a slightly tarnished, but decent knight.

"What happened afterward?"

"She stayed there while I ran back to the house and got the

money. I'd been doing odd jobs around the house for years, saving up to buy a car for college. My dad believed implicitly that young men should work for what they wanted."

"And it wasn't in the bank?"

"Our house was a fortress. I kept my earnings in a small wall safe in my bedroom."

"How much?" Gillian asked.

"I went back and handed her seven thousand dollars in cash."

"Please tell me she didn't take it."

His mouth was grim. "Oh, yes. She took it. And I never saw either her or her husband again."

"Do you think they deliberately set you up?"

"I don't know for sure. I've thought about it a million times over the years. I think it just happened. And with the money in hand, they took off. It's possible she even stayed with him."

A hint of nausea returned. Gillian knew without Devlyn saying the words that his first sexual experience had been tainted with guilt because of the woman's marital status. He had been seduced, plain and simple. Even if it truly was a spontaneous act on the woman's part, it was a terrible thing to do to a young boy.

"So what happened when you went off to college?"

A long silence ensued. Then Devlyn sighed. "Honest to God? I was scared. It occurred to me that I hadn't used a condom. So disease was a possibility. And there was even a chance that I had fathered a child. For months I lived in fear that she would show up on my doorstep."

Gillian scooted closer and wrapped an arm across his chest. "I'm so sorry. She took your innocence."

"Yeah, but what eighteen-year-old guy wants to be innocent?"

The words were flip, but she could hear the hurt that lingered, even now, more than a decade later. "But you found a girlfriend eventually?"

"Not a girlfriend. More like a series of one-night stands, mostly after keg parties." He covered her hand with his. "I was smart enough to use protection every time, but that was about the only bit of intelligence I exhibited. I lost count of how many girls I screwed the next two years."

Gillian didn't know what to say. He wasn't the only guy to sleep his way through college. But she sensed that the experience was a dark spot in his soul. Or he wouldn't be telling her in such detail. "You said two years...what happened after that?"

"I wised up...woke up one day in some dorm room I didn't recognize, and I realized that I'd had enough. Three months later, I met Tammi."

"Tammi?" He had said her name with affection.

"We met in an upper-level business class. I was doing advanced work. Tammi was a senior. The professor assigned a project and made us partners."

"And you fell in love with her."

Devlyn's chest rose and fell as he laughed. "Who's telling this story? You, or me? No, I didn't fall in love. But for the first time in my life, I had a female friend. It was novel, but nice. Tammi helped straighten out my head a little bit."

"Did you ever sleep with her?"

"Once, right before she graduated. But there were no fireworks. It was a bittersweet goodbye, nothing more than that. I hear from her now and again. She's a stay-at-home mom with three kids."

The little lick of jealousy Gillian experienced was unfounded, but real. And at that moment she realized the danger Devlyn represented. Already he had disarmed her with his painfully frank recitation. She wanted to hold him, to make up for the past.

But Devlyn Wolff was a grown man. And he didn't need Gillian's sympathy. What he wanted…apparently…was a convenient affair.

She got to her feet, wobbling only slightly. "Shouldn't the car be here by now?"

Devlyn stood as well, frowning. "That's all you're going to say? After I poured my heart out to you?"

She wrapped her arms around her waist, her stomach clenching with faint memories of her gastric distress. "You're trying to convince me that it would be fun to fool around while I'm working with you."

"Did I succeed?" That wicked, flashing grin was back.

"I'll consider it. You're a handsome man with a quirky sense of humor. And I'll be living in a town where the pool of eligible men is almost nonexistent. So maybe. But don't push. My mother works for your family. I'm not sure how I feel about that. Give me time to think about it."

"Fair enough." He smoothed her hair from her face, making her pulse stumble. "How about a kiss…just one…so we can test the waters."

"I'm not kissing you after I puked my guts out. That's not the kind of first impression a woman wants to make."

"Believe me. Guys aren't that picky. But in honor of your meticulous hygiene, how about I avoid your mouth?"

She took a step backward. "No." Devlyn Wolff touching her anywhere seemed like a really bad idea.

He circled her wrist with one big hand, his thumb on her pulse. "Relax, Gillian. I can't do anything to you out here in the open."

But that was a lie. He reeled her in, not stopping until her breasts were against his chest. She could either crane her neck to see his expression or rest her cheek on warm, starchy cotton that smelled like Devlyn. It was no choice at all.

Their heights were a good match. She fit nicely in his embrace. "Go ahead and do it," she said. "You're making me nervous."

He laughed. "Whatever the lady wants."

Nudging her head to one side, he nibbled his way from her ear to her shoulder. Gooseflesh erupted everywhere his teeth grazed her sensitive skin. When her knees began to tremble, her arms went around his neck for support.

Then it was no problem at all to return the naughty love bites Devlyn was inflicting. But when the tip of her tongue traced his throat at the opening of his shirt, he released her abruptly and staggered backward several steps.

He held out his hand. "I think we'll call that experiment a success." His cheeks were ruddy and his chest heaved.

In the distance a car horn tooted.

"Is that our ride?" Gillian turned, not sure if she was relieved or disappointed.

Two dark SUVs pulled up at the edge of the field. There was not much of a shoulder, so the vehicles were partway in the road.

Devlyn started grabbing up stuff. "C'mon. Let's not keep them waiting."

They tramped across the field rapidly, but Gillian held back when Devlyn chatted with the drivers. The sun was very low, casting lengthy shadows across the land. Would Devlyn still want to show her the property after dark? Surely not.

He turned and motioned. "I can send you back up the mountain with the guys, but if you feel like it, I'd like you to join me for dinner with an investor. I stood him up last night after you played pinball with that tree."

"I'll go back to the house." *And do what?* she wondered. Staying at the castle was really an awkward arrangement. Perhaps she could get her mom to come pick her up for the evening or ask one of Devlyn's drivers to take her directly to her mother's.

Devlyn frowned, evidently not hearing the answer he wanted. "Come with me," he cajoled. "He was really angry when I didn't show. You'll be proof that my Boy Scout good deed was the right thing to do. And besides…you're on the clock, remember?"

"That's not fair."

He grinned and opened the passenger door of the car he was preparing to drive, motioning for her to get in. "Dinner's on me."

She shook her head in mock disgust. "You must have been spoiled rotten as a kid."

His smile dimmed. "Let's just say that I like getting what I want."

She slid in beside him, conscious that her only hope of escape was driving away in the opposite direction. "And so do I. So one of us is doomed to disappointment."

Devlyn drove in silence, rethinking his strategy with Gillian. Perhaps having her at the castle wasn't the best idea. His family would be bound to notice if he started having sleepovers. And Gillian's mother was not likely to appreciate the son of her employer hanging around.

Life would be a lot easier if he could simply spirit Gillian away to his multimillion-dollar rooftop condo in Atlanta. But the job he had hired her to do was real. And needed to be done in and around Burton. Which meant that if Devlyn wanted to explore this surprising and compelling physical attraction, he was going to have to stay on the mountain much longer than he had originally intended.

He'd never had much respect for entrepreneurs who allowed pleasure to get in the way of business. But damned if Devlyn hadn't just entangled the two without the slightest bit of regret.

They pulled up in front of the restaurant in Charlottesville with five minutes to spare. Gillian fussed with her hair. "I'm not really dressed for a place like this."

"Don't worry," he said, handing his keys to the valet. "It's pretty dark inside."

"Very funny."

Horatio Clement was already seated. The man was a long-time family friend, at least a decade older than Victor and Vincent. He was a bachelor, had a stock portfolio that would make Bill Gates weep and was as tightfisted as Scrooge.

Devlyn's job was to cajole him into loosening the purse strings long enough to invest a healthy chunk of cash into Wolff Enterprises' latest expansion…a brand-new headquarters in Mexico City. With locations already on the West Coast and in London and Paris, the Wolffs owned a sizable chunk of real estate…high-tech offices that oversaw a multitude of interests from railroads to television stations to manufacturing.

Devlyn put his hand at Gillian's back, ushering her forward. "Hello, Horatio," he said. "I was hoping you wouldn't mind some feminine company this evening."

Horatio's bushy white eyebrows lifted. "Not your usual style, is she, Devvie boy?" He turned toward Gillian. "What's your name, girl?"

She shook his bony hand. "Gillian Carlyle. And you've hit the nail on the head, sir. I'm definitely not his type. But he's feeling guilty for running me off the road last night. That's why he missed your dinner appointment."

Devlyn ground his teeth. "I did *not* run you off the road. You were going way too fast."

Horatio snorted. "I've seen you drive, kid. I choose to believe this nice young woman."

Devlyn had no choice but to sit down and nurse his wounds. Before he could get the ball rolling, Gillian and Horatio were thick as thieves, the old man spinning one outrageous tale after the other, and Gillian egging him on with her contagious laughter.

It was going to be a long night.

Eight

Gillian hadn't expected to enjoy dinner, but Horatio was a darling. He had a snap in his eyes and a tart, wry humor that kept her on the verge of laughter as they dined on filet mignon, baby asparagus and giant, fluffy baked potatoes.

Devlyn spoke little, his expression hard to read. At one point, she stood and excused herself. "I know you gentlemen have business to discuss. I'm going to visit the ladies' room and then call and check on my mother."

When she returned five minutes later, Devlyn's face was a thundercloud, and Horatio had his arms crossed over his chest. The older of the two waved at Gillian. "I have some questions for you, young lady. Would you do business with him if you were me?"

Gillian hesitated. "I don't know all that much about finances…but I do know that Devlyn has a brilliant financial mind. Why else would his father and his uncle give him control of the company at his young age? My guess is that your investment will grow rapidly."

"Or it will disappear like smoke in the wind if this damned economy gets any worse."

"You can't take it with you, sir."

Devlyn froze. Had Gillian really said that?

For a split second nobody moved. Then Horatio threw back his head and roared with laughter. "This one's a pistol, Devvie. You'd better hang on to her."

Devlyn, accustomed to smooth-talking his way out of any situation, didn't know what to say.

Gillian stepped in like a seasoned negotiator. "With all that money you're going to make, I have a proposition for you."

Horatio eyed her sadly. "The doc says my ticker isn't strong enough to take those little blue pills. But I'm flattered, darlin'."

Gillian actually blushed. "Behave yourself. I'll bet you were a lot like Devlyn when you were his age. You loved the challenge of besting an opponent…the adrenaline rush. But that doesn't mean you have to walk away from the table. Say yes, Horatio. You know you want to."

The old man took a sip of his seventy-five-dollar bottle of wine. He stared at Devlyn. "I'll give you every cent I've got if I can have your little woman."

Devlyn scowled. "Not for sale, sir. And FYI, that request is politically incorrect."

"I'm eighty-six years old. I can say whatever the hell I want." But he patted Gillian's hand. "Sorry, sweetheart. No disrespect intended. You'll forgive an old man, won't you?"

She squeezed his gnarled fingers. "Of course. Now do you want to hear my proposition or not?"

His eyes twinkled. "Go for it."

"I don't know if you've heard, but the Wolff family is giving our little town of Burton an elementary school, K–8. We've never had one, and our children, even the youngest ones, have to ride the bus a long way every morning and afternoon. Why don't you donate several hundred thousand dollars toward the project, and we'll name the school after you."

She shot a worried look at Devlyn. "Can we do that?"

He sighed, fully aware that his business meeting had gotten entirely out of hand. "Sure. But he's supposed to be giving *me* money, not you."

Gillian waved a hand. "There's plenty to go around. Now be honest, Horatio. Wouldn't you like to leave behind a legacy that will benefit hundreds of children, maybe thousands in the long run? And you can be a consultant."

"Now wait a minute." Devlyn felt a noose tightening around his neck. It was happening again. He tried to help a woman in need, and suddenly his life was flying out of control. "I just hired *you,*" he said, pointing at Gillian. "I can't afford another employee."

Horatio grinned, enjoying Devlyn's discomfiture. "I'll work for a dollar a day...and dinner once a week with Gillian. Alone."

"Five dollars a day, and no hanky-panky with my girlfriend."

Gillian's lips pursed. "I'm not your girlfriend. Office relationships seldom work out."

"We don't have an office...unless you want to go to Atlanta with me."

"Too far. I suppose I'll simply have to make do. Thank you, Mr. Clement. I think we have a deal. But you and Devlyn still have to agree on the Mexico thing."

Horatio shook his head. "It's a sad day when a grown man has to bring in a female to help shake down an old man. I'll be lucky to have enough left to pay for a nursing home."

Gillian's face fell. "I certainly don't expect you to jeopardize your own health and well-being, Horatio. I was presumptuous about the school. Close the deal with Devlyn. Don't worry about anything else."

Devlyn sighed. "He's kidding, Gillian. This *poor old man* could buy the state of Virginia if it was for sale. Don't waste time worrying about him."

Gillian glared. "Show some respect to your elders."

Horatio hopped into the conversation. "Yeah, Devlyn. Kiss my as—"

Gillian held up a hand. "Enough. Both of you are acting like children. Sign the darned papers and let's be done with this."

"We don't have any papers here," Devlyn said. "This is a gentleman's agreement, right, Horatio?"

Horatio stuck out his hand. "Let's get it over with, boy. Before she nags us to death. That's why women are no good in business."

Devlyn and Gillian groaned in unison.

Horatio managed to look innocent. "What did I say?"

Devlyn shook his adversary's hand and waved at the waiter for the check. "You're a scoundrel and a crook. But thank you, Horatio. You won't regret this."

Gillian learned a lot about Devlyn that evening. He could have conducted the same meeting at a boring office in thirty minutes. But instead, he'd taken the time to wine and dine a lonely octogenarian. And unless Gillian was mistaken, Devlyn enjoyed the mock battle as much as Horatio did.

In the car on the way back to the castle, a hushed silence reigned. Gillian didn't want to sleep under Devlyn Wolff's roof. And did he expect her to occupy the same suite as last night? The one with the connecting door to his room?

Perhaps agreeing to work with him had been a bad idea, but what choice did she have? It went against the grain to mooch off her hardworking mother, and any openings at area schools would likely only become available at the end of the year.

"How long have you known Horatio?" she asked, uneasy about Devlyn's mood. He was gregarious to a fault, so now that he was sober and quiet, she had to wonder what he was thinking.

He shot her a sideways glance, his gaze trained on the road ahead. "My earliest memory of Horatio comes from my fifth birthday party. He gave me a pony. Told me that a boy my age should learn how to ride a horse. I was petrified and determined not to show it. Horatio drove up the mountain once a week for six months until he was sure I could handle riding without getting hurt."

"He must love you very much."

"Yeah…beneath that crusty exterior, he's a teddy bear. But only in his personal life. He raised hell when he was still working."

"Did he ever have a family of his own?"

"He was married…when he was very young. My dad told me Horatio's wife died in childbirth. The two men had that in common, the loss of a spouse. I think that's why they became friends outside of the business setting. Horatio never found anyone else he could love like he loved his wife, so he's been on his own ever since."

"That seems so sad."

"He's not a hermit or a miser. He lives life. But he keeps her memory as a shrine."

"And your father…I know he and your uncle never remarried, but did they date at all…or have women friends?"

"If they did, I never knew it. They devoted themselves to my siblings, my cousins and me, to our safety, our education, our happiness. It wasn't always a smooth road. Dad and Uncle Vic suffered in the aftermath of the tragedy. In ways I was too young to understand. But they were determined that no harm would come to us."

"You were a lucky child."

"Indeed."

Despite the fact that he agreed with her, some intonation in his voice suggested bleak irony. She'd been around enough to witness his privileged lifestyle. And despite the constraints of being held a virtual captive on his mountain, it was still pretty great. The affairs of the Wolffs were generally known in Burton, but were there secrets to which she wasn't privy? "So what about you, Devlyn? Your cousins have started getting married. Will you be next?"

"Is that an offer?"

"Don't flatter yourself. You're way too bossy and stubborn."

"Pot. Kettle."

"I'll give you that one. We do share a few similar traits. But I have no desire to conquer the world one stock option at a time. I like what I do…being a teacher, I mean."

"Some people can't imagine shutting themselves up in a room for six or seven hours every day with twenty-five kids."

"I love them," she said simply. "And I love knowing that what I'm doing makes a real difference."

"And what about your personal life?"

"I already told you. I'll get married, I hope. I'd love to have a big family, maybe three or four kids. What about you? Tell me about your ideal woman."

"She's meek, brings me my slippers and agrees with everything I say."

Gillian laughed. "It's amazing you manage to get any female companionship at all. Of course the money and your looks account for some of it."

"I'm flattered."

"Don't be. Those are both negatives in my book."

"Says the woman who was unemployed just yesterday."

"Wow. You don't mind hitting below the belt."

"You're the one who said I'm not worth chasing."

"I said you weren't *husband* material. No woman wants a guy who's going to get hit on by all the PTA and soccer moms."

"Was there actually a compliment buried in there somewhere?"

They reached the bottom of the mountain and passed through the security gates. Gillian felt a squiggle of panic as they slid shut behind them. No way out…

"I'll be the first to admit that you're handsome and charming and probably the life of the party."

"But…?"

"I think I'm more suited to a nine-to-five banker with thinning hair."

He negotiated a hairpin curve with ease. "Should I feel threatened? Have you met this paragon of boredom?"

"Not yet. But I have a little time. You still haven't answered my question. When do *you* plan to marry and settle down?"

It was too dark now to see his expression. Tall trees flanked the road, blocking any ambient light.

"I don't. The business is my baby. My entire family trusts me to keep Wolff Enterprises profitable. It's an all-consuming job. I'd be a lousy husband and father."

His words were brusque, the tone flat. Something odd ran beneath the surface.

"Busy people get married all the time and raise families. Don't you want to carry on the Wolff name?"

"I have one brother and three cousins to do that. Drop it, Gillian."

She subsided into silence, disturbed by the notion that his vehement repudiation of marriage and fatherhood was something more than a bachelor's off-the-cuff aversion to commitment. But he'd made it clear that the topic wasn't open for discussion.

They pulled up beneath a stone portico and an employee took the vehicle away to be parked in one of the garages behind and below the main house. Gillian stood uncertainly, feeling a return of her earlier misgivings. She and Devlyn had not defined their working relationship. And for someone who planned her classroom activities to the minute, the lack of structure was extremely uncomfortable.

He shepherded her inside, leading her without words toward a part of the house she hadn't seen in years. "I want to show you something," he said. "Maybe it will help you understand why I want you to work with me on the school."

The room they entered was lined with file cabinets and a series of wall safes. Along another long expanse, a sophisticated computer setup blinked lazily. Devlyn went to one of the safes in the middle, punched in a code and opened the small metal door. Removing a box, he motioned for her to sit.

The room was not meant for relaxation. Her only option was one of two straight-backed office chairs. She perched there and stared at him. "What is it?"

His face impassive, he extracted a small item and handed it to her. Her stomach turned over. It was a child's clumsy attempt at a greeting card, at least a quarter of a century old. The edges of the paper were ragged with age.

She bit her lips, opening the missive carefully. As if it were yesterday, she remembered sitting at the kitchen table in her house, laboring over the complicated series of letters. "You kept this? But you were so angry."

He sat beside her. "After you left that day, I took it home. For some reason, I found comfort in it. I never showed it to anyone. I didn't want to be teased. You think I offered you a job because you needed one. And I did. It's serendipitous that someone with your skills and know-how is available to help us with the school. But most of all I wanted to say thank you."

"You don't owe me anything, Devlyn. My mother probably made me do that card for you."

"Doesn't matter. The point is that you reached out to me, and even though it's a bit overdue, I want you to know how much I appreciated it…still do, as a matter of fact."

He slid a hand beneath her hair, cupping her neck. "I know all the reasons we shouldn't get involved. You have weird hang-ups about your mother working here. I'm not a man who will give you babies and a minivan…and we face an appalling lack of privacy for what I have in mind. But fate has brought you back into my life, and I want you." He bent his head and found her lips in a warm, insistent, teasing kiss.

She tried to say his name, but he took her breath with his irresistible, coaxing mouth.

"Give me a chance, Gillian," he muttered. "Give *us* a chance."

Nine

Devlyn was pushing her. He knew it. And it wasn't his MO at all. He'd never had problems getting women. Much of the time, he had to shoo them away.

But Gillian did something to him. Perhaps it was because she had known him as a boy, had witnessed and understood most of the ins and outs of his life. The ups and downs. When he was with her he experienced a feeling of nostalgia, of peace.

When her lips moved beneath his, responding hesitantly, peace was the last thing on his mind. He groaned, deepening the kiss without conscious thought, plumbing the sweet depths of her mouth with his tongue, sinking his teeth into her bottom lip.

The position was awkward, both of them side by side in hard chairs. And the door was unlocked. All these realities flitted through his brain, even as his erection hardened painfully. "Come to my room," he muttered. "Please."

Gillian didn't say anything, perhaps because he wasn't allowing her to come up for air. Again and again he kissed her, his heart pounding and his head swimming. He was reaching the point of no return when Gillian put a hand on his chest.

"We have to stop, Devlyn. This isn't the place."

Even if the words were hoarse, they still had that schoolmarm tone that for some inexplicable reason turned him on. "That's why we're going to my room. Or hell, yours. I don't care." He cupped one breast in his fingers. Barely a handful. And yet the rush of tenderness that overwhelmed him only made him want her more.

She whimpered and pressed nearer, sending a rush of excitement like a tidal wave through his chest. Gillian wanted him. No doubt about it. But when he put his hand under her sweater, feeling the silk of bare skin, she shoved him away. "Enough."

It was sufficient to shock him back to his senses. The sound of voices in the hall made him curse. "I'm sorry. You make me crazy."

She cocked her head, straightening her hair with hands that trembled. "Why? I've seen pictures of the women you date… in society columns, in magazines, online. They're all tall and blonde and medically enhanced in the bosom."

"No one says bosom anymore."

"Answer me," she said.

It was the trace of hurt in her eyes that did him in. He rubbed his thumb over her bottom lip, its plump curve still damp from his kisses. "Aw, hell, Gillian. You've got something none of them have."

"What?" The vulnerability in her gaze belied the air of confidence that he usually saw in her.

He shrugged. "You belong here. You're part of Wolff Mountain. And that makes me feel…" He stumbled to a halt, not even sure what he was talking about.

At that moment, the door opened and Devlyn's father walked in. "I wondered where you were. How was the dinner? Did Horatio jerk you around?"

Devlyn rose, pulling Gillian to her feet as well, hoping he had his body under control. "He tried. Dad...this is Doreen Carlyle's daughter, Gillian. I'm sure you remember her. She used to spend time here when her mom was working."

Vincent Wolff was no fool. He stepped forward, hand outstretched. "Glad to see you, Gillian. I suppose you know that your mother is a valuable part of our staff."

"Thank you, sir. It's nice to see you again."

Vincent's gaze went from Gillian to his son and back again. Devlyn was pretty sure his father realized what he had interrupted, but he didn't do anything to embarrass Gillian.

"Did you need something, Dad?"

Vincent nodded. "I do. We need to talk about a labor issue I just got wind of in France. But it can wait."

Gillian slid past Devlyn toward the door. "You two go ahead. It's been a long day, and I think I'll go to my room. I assume it's the same one."

Devlyn tried to communicate his displeasure, but she was looking at his father. "Gillian, I'll bring you up-to-date on the school plan in the morning. Nine o'clock sharp."

She gave him a cool stare, one designed to put him in his place. "Yes, sir. I'll be there."

When the door closed, leaving Devlyn and his father alone, Vincent Wolff eyed his son with a gaze that revealed little of what he was thinking. Devlyn turned his back, feigning nonchalance, and scooped up the childish note as if it were nothing important. When he had returned it to the safe, he faced his father once again.

"What's the deal with Paris? I talked to the head of Human Resources last week and everything sounded fine."

"Forget about Paris. I want to know why that girl was here overnight."

Devlyn tensed, unused to being on the defensive with his father. As a rule, they got along really well. "She wrecked her car. Her mother was out of town. I thought she should stay until morning in case she had any residual effects."

"And how does that explain why I saw her suitcase a moment ago in one of our most beautiful guest suites, the one that happens to connect with yours?"

"I told you. I hired her. And I thought it would be more efficient to have her on-site since I'm juggling the Atlanta office, as well."

"You told me *you* were going to move in, not her. I've seen that look in your eyes," his father said quietly. "Gillian Carlyle is not one of your high-class, couture-clad socialites. She's a bright, levelheaded woman, but she's no match for you."

"You don't understand."

"So explain it to me."

"I like her."

"And?"

"And nothing."

"You're well beyond needing my approval of your bed partners, if you ever did. But I'm telling you right now. Don't mess with Gillian. All ethical considerations aside, your behavior could open us up to a lawsuit since her mother is on staff. It's too messy. Find someone else to entertain you while you're here."

"Nothing is going on."

"I saw your face when I opened the door. You want her. But you can't have her."

"That's between Gillian and me."

His father sat down in a chair, his face marked with fatigue. The sudden change in expression alarmed Devlyn. "You okay, Dad? Is it your heart?"

Vincent closed his eyes and inhaled, holding his breath for several seconds before releasing the air.

"It's not my heart. This chorus line of girlfriends you juggle is never going to change until you face the truth. We need to talk about your mother, Devvie."

Devlyn turned to stone, his heart still beating, but every muscle and sinew in his body rigid with emotional agony. "No, we don't. Not today. Not ever."

"I swear I didn't know, Devvie. Not until long after she was gone. I was working crazy hours, making money like a madman, and I missed what was happening under my nose. I'm so sorry, son."

Devlyn's lungs screamed for air. His legs barely supported him. Unwittingly, his father had resurrected Devlyn's own fears. Devlyn wasn't worthy of a relationship with a decent woman like Gillian. He was damaged goods. "It's in the past. Forget it." Wheeling around like a cornered animal, he bolted through the door.

Gillian unpacked her small suitcase and put her things in an antique bureau lined with delicate tissue scented with lilacs. The fragrance reminded her of the large bushes that bloomed alongside the castle driveway in spring.

After a phone call to her mother and another one to her closest teacher friend in Charlottesville, she found herself at loose ends. The flat-screen TV in the armoire held little interest, and the book she'd brought with her had hit a dull spot.

And then it came to her…she could revisit the library. Surely it would be empty at this time of night, and she remembered the way there, so she could hopefully go unnoticed.

She changed into soft, faded jeans and a long-sleeve cashmere blend sweater. Wearing thick, warm socks, she padded shoeless down the halls and through the corridors until she came to the room where she had spent so many happy times as a child.

The distinctive aroma of old books and pipe smoke drifted out as she hovered on the threshold. Smiling with delight, she slipped inside and quietly closed the door. With Devlyn, earlier, she'd been too on edge to enjoy her surroundings. Now she absorbed it all. Nothing had changed. With a little imagination, she could see herself at seven or eight, curled up in the window seat reading *Winnie-the-Pooh* or *The Secret Garden*.

She had been an excellent student, but shy and with few friends. Most of the kids in her grade lived in populated areas some distance from Burton. Gillian had always felt the sting of being different. As an only child, she didn't even have siblings for playmates.

Tiptoeing to avoid detection, she browsed the shelves. Someone had left a dim light burning, so there was just enough illumination to read titles. She stroked her hand over the leather spines. Victor and Vincent Wolff had amassed an incredible collection over the years. Art. Biography. Philosophy. History. A broad array of fiction. And of course, business. But it was the juvenile books that caught her eye. Several of them she vividly remembered reading...*The Velveteen Rabbit. Adventures of Huckleberry Finn. Little Women.*

On those times when Gillian had dug in her heels and refused to go to the castle after her encounter with Devlyn, Doreen had sometimes found a sitter, a neighbor, a friend. But she always brought home an armful of stories to be devoured and later returned.

Little Gillian adored books. Grown-up Gillian was equally enchanted. She found a worn copy of *Charlotte's Web* and took it with her to a burgundy, velvet-covered sofa flanking the empty fireplace. She would have preferred the cushioned window seat, but she wasn't willing to turn on anything brighter than the small lamp with the Tiffany shade that sat on a piecrust table at her elbow.

She loved the lamp. The mauves and greens and blues of the dragonflies almost seemed to glow. Settling into the cushions with a sigh of happiness, she began turning pages.

Devlyn wanted to run. He did, in fact, plunge into the forest and stumble as fast as his legs would take him down one of the many trails that crisscrossed the mountaintop. He thought about climbing in his car and driving fast as hell back to the anonymity of Atlanta where he was the boss and no one dared cross him. Where he could hide out in his sleek, impersonally decorated condo and forget about things he'd worked a lifetime not to remember.

But what would he do about Gillian? Send her down the mountain with no explanation? In the dark?

Damn it.

A rogue branch snagged his shoulder, ripping his shirt. The pain snapped him out of his downward spiral. He leaned against a huge tree, bent forward at the waist and bowed his head, hands on his knees, gasping for air.

All he could think about was seeing her…seeing Gillian. He gave himself a few minutes to regain his equilibrium, to put the monster back in the box. Nothing had happened. Nothing had changed. His dad might suspect, but no one knew for sure what demons lurked inside him. His defenses were intact. There was no reason for alarm. Slowly, he made his way back to the house.

Finding her room empty was a shock. The door to the hallway stood ajar a couple of inches. "Gillian?" He called her name several times, loud enough for her to hear if she was in the bathroom. But no answer. Where was she?

It took him thirty minutes to find her, his impatience increasing exponentially with every tick of the clock. He knew the huge, sprawling house from cellar to attic. His first guess was the warm, comfy kitchen...then the twenty-seat movie theater...finally the exercise room.

As he stood in the front foyer, grinding his teeth in frustration, suddenly it came to him. Little Gillian Carlyle spent many hours in one particular room. The library. He couldn't believe he hadn't thought of it before now.

When he got there, out of breath from his sudden sprint, the door was firmly shut. Was he wrong? Hoping not to startle her if she was inside, he gently turned the knob.

Shadows filled the room. The walls were lined with shelves that reached the ceiling. Many a time he had sailed one way and another on the moving staircase, despite remonstrations from his father. But less pleasant memories intruded.

This was also the room where he and his siblings and cousins had been given their lessons. Not allowed to attend regular schools because of the fear of kidnapping, all six children had been instructed in this room by a series of tutors...even in the summer. Victor and Vincent Wolff had high expectations for their offspring.

The worst times were the sunny, warm days. The pleasant library had become a prison. For a boy with energy to burn and an insatiable curiosity, having to finish lessons when the world outside beckoned had been little less than torture.

He shook off the memories and eyed his reason for coming. Gillian was asleep on the love seat, sitting up, her legs propped on a low coffee table. She had been reading. A book lay open in her hands, but her head had fallen to one side, her mouth curved in a faint smile.

Carefully, he sat down beside her and eased her into a reclining position, her head in his lap. She murmured something in her sleep, but didn't wake. A bruise on her cheekbone reminded him that she was surely still stiff and sore from the accident.

For a fleeting second he imagined what it would have been like had he found her dead in that car. The possibility chilled his blood. He would never have had a chance to apologize, but even worse than that, he could never have known the adult Gillian, with her prickly ways and her quiet charm.

Gently, he stroked her hair, fingers skimming now and again over the bruise. It troubled him, marring her creamy skin and reminding him that life was fleeting. God knew he and his family had learned that lesson the hard way. Because of the shared tragedy, over the years the Wolff clan had grown ever closer, a bulwark for each other against those who would seek to destroy them.

Gillian stirred and stretched. Then she froze when she realized where she was…and with whom. "Devlyn?"

"Never try to hide from a Wolff," he said, teasing her. "I'll always find you."

Ten

Gillian realized several things simultaneously. Devlyn's hand was under her sweater. She hadn't put on a bra when she'd changed clothes. And his fingers were tracing her ribs one at a time, higher and higher.

"I thought you were talking to your dad." The words came out on an embarrassing squeak.

His chest rose and fell on a sigh. "I was. We're done."

"He doesn't want me here, does he?"

"No. But not for the reasons you think."

Her stomach curled in embarrassment. "I'll go in the morning."

"No, you won't. We have work to do."

"The house belongs to your father and uncle. You're only visiting. It's not really your place to invite me to move in."

"It's my home, too. And besides, Dad's reservations would still exist even if you were staying at your mother's house."

"So he doesn't think I'm qualified to help with the new

school, is that it?" She'd suspected the job seemed too good to be true. And maybe it was. She didn't want to be beholden to the Wolffs. If her services weren't needed, she should go.

When she tried to sit up, Devlyn stopped her by the simple expedient of holding his large hand, fingers splayed, against her belly. "My dad trusts me to hire competent people."

"But?"

"He's worried that I'll seduce you and break your heart."

Vincent Wolff was astute. Even now, Gillian's emotions were dangerously involved. She looked into Devlyn's eyes and saw past the sophisticated man to the faint remnants of a vulnerable boy. Everything inside her strained toward him, ached to assuage his hurt and his guilt. Despite recognizing the risks, Gillian acknowledged in that one fraught moment that she wanted to become Devlyn's lover, for as long as it lasted.

Did that make her a bad person? Or even worse, hopelessly naive? "What did you tell him?"

"I said it was between us."

Devlyn had worn dress slacks to the meeting with Horatio. Unlike Gillian, he'd not taken the time to change. Beside her cheek, beneath the thin fabric, his sex was swollen, hard. If Gillian turned her head, her lips would be able to caress the length of him.

She had come to the moment of truth. A turning point that would require an odd combination of pragmatism and confidence. It was no decision at all. She took his hand and deliberately moved it upward to cover her breast. The connection of his palm to her sensitive flesh was electric. Devlyn groaned, his fingers tightening momentarily. Gillian experienced a rush of heat and desperate hunger that left her breathless.

Their eyes met. She reached up to touch his cheek. "It's okay," she said. "I know this is what it is. I want you anyway."

His expression was troubled, but his fingertips teased her

nipple as if they had a mind of their own. "I'll never lie to you, Gillian."

"I know." It wasn't him she worried about. He had been very clear about his motives, his plans for the future. Gillian would have to be the one to step back if she found herself in deep water. She wouldn't allow her heart to be broken. She was smarter than that.

"I love your skin," he muttered. "You're soft, so soft." Now both of his hands made mischief. She cried out when he pinched the tips of her aching breasts simultaneously and tugged. Fire shot from the point of contact to a place deep in her womb and below.

Her thighs clenched. "We need to move. To your bedroom." She was barely able to construct a coherent thought.

"Everyone's asleep. I'll lock the door." He slid from beneath her, and she felt his loss like a physical pain.

He was gone fleeting seconds. When he returned, she was standing up. She launched herself into his arms, delighting in the easy strength he displayed. She was neither tall nor short, but he pulled her to his chest and lifted her off her feet long enough to destroy her with a kiss that communicated yearning, masculine intent and heart-melting, disarming gentleness.

"Take off your shirt," she said. "I want to see you."

He chuckled at her urgency. "Bossy, bossy, bossy." But he obeyed, unbuttoning the top few buttons with maddening deliberation and then dragging the garment over his head and tossing it aside.

Her legs felt funny, like the time she had downed a glass of Long Island Iced Tea, not knowing what it was. But tonight she was stone-cold sober. And Devlyn Wolff was responsible for her sexual inebriation.

She put her hands on his wide shoulders, testing the resiliency of his skin, absorbing the warmth and power of muscle and sinew over bone. He stood rigid, his hands at his sides.

"You're so beautiful," she said, moving her hands across his broad chest. The light covering of hair made him look more primitive than the man she knew as a brilliant businessman. Half-naked, he exuded a force of will that thrilled even as it terrified.

She tasted one flat, copper-colored nipple. His whole body trembled. And still he didn't touch her. Her hands went to his belt. "May I?"

"Knock yourself out." It was a weak attempt at humor. The skin on his face stretched tightly over his cheekbones, his eyes squeezed shut as if he couldn't bear to watch her learning the planes of his body.

Clumsily, almost paralyzed by shyness, she unfastened his belt and drew it slowly through the belt loops. Her fingers settled on the tab of his zipper and stopped. His erection flexed against her touch, almost as if it were begging for her attention.

Devlyn grabbed her wrist. "No more. Not yet. I can't take it."

He went from passive to domineering so quickly, she was stunned. He grabbed handfuls of her sweater and dragged it over her head. Then he stopped, staring at her chest. "Sweet heaven. You're beautiful, Gillian. So damned beautiful."

He walked her backward until he could sit down, urging her forward to straddle his lap. She settled on top of him, leaned forward and put her hands on his shoulders. "Don't we have too many clothes on?"

"There you go again." He nuzzled his face in the valley between her breasts as if to reinforce the fact that he was teasing her. "Relax, honey. I'm in charge here."

She could have pressed the point. Sex was a two-way street. But in truth, she had no reason to doubt his ability to take over. When his mouth covered one aching nipple, brushing it repeatedly with his tongue and teeth, the rational part of her brain shut down. *Dear God.*

All that remained were the pleasure receptors. And they were in danger of overload. In her imagination, she had pictured Devlyn taking her hard and fast, demonstrating the same dominating force he wielded in the boardroom.

But she hadn't even been close. He treated her body as if it were a rare discovery, mapping it one sector at a time. Time was irrelevant. Devlyn feasted on her with the relish of a man coming off months of deprivation.

From her waist to her breasts, to the tender skin beneath and behind her ear, he kissed, he licked, he nipped, he stroked. Her breaths came in sharp pants, need building to the point of pain. "Please," she croaked. "I want more."

Unfastening the button at the top of her zipper, he slid both hands down inside her jeans beneath her panties and stroked her ass. "I think we're done with these," he said, his words guttural and harsh.

Pushing her to her feet, he dragged the denim down her legs, taking care to leave her lacy bikini in place. She wrapped her arms around her breasts, stricken by a return of shyness. She had been in relationships before. But never had she felt so exposed, so vulnerable.

Devlyn scooted to the edge of the sofa, cupping his hand over her mound. Slowly, making her want to scream in frustration, he began to finger her, sliding his thumb back and forth over the damp crotch of her underwear. She pressed her aching sex into his palm, begging wordlessly for release.

But he had a plan. One from which he would not stray. Curling his fist around the thin side of the bikini underpants, he stretched them so that he could drag the fabric back and forth across her most sensitive spot. The shock of it made heat pool in the place between her legs that ached so terribly. She writhed, moving closer. "Devlyn…"

Now he entered her with two fingers, not moving or thrusting. Merely letting her experience the mimicry of what was to come. She was wild with need, panting in her desperation. His thumb brushed the tiny nerve center that throbbed and burned, and she cried out, slammed by a climax that left her with no place to hide, no modesty, no maidenly dissimulation.

His arms were around her, supporting her as she rode out the last vestiges of pleasure. Limp and helpless, she barely had enough stamina to remain standing.

And then he started all over again.

Her panties disappeared in a flash. His arms encircled her hips, positioning his mouth at her center. "Again," he muttered. "I want you to come again."

Feeling him taste her so intimately was like nothing she had ever experienced. The rough pressure of his tongue, combined with the swollen remains of her last orgasm, brought her to the peak in record time. She tangled her hands in his hair, holding on as the insistent tide threatened to drag her under.

Shuddering and speechless, she clung to his shoulders. He stood and lifted her, stretching her out on the sofa. With jerky movements, he ripped off his pants and boxers and kicked them off with his shoes and socks. Foggy with the aftermath of what he had done to her, for her, she gazed up at him. He was primed and ready, his erection eager, bold.

"I want to touch you," she said.

He came down beside her, wedging his hips between her thighs. Leaning on one arm, he smiled. "I'm all yours."

She curled her fingers around his shaft, noting the way he winced as she did so. "Too hard?"

He grimaced. "Not hard enough." He nudged her legs apart even more, preparing to enter her, and then he cursed long and low.

"What? What's wrong?"

"No condom," he growled, his expression fierce.

She wanted him so desperately she couldn't think of anything but feeling him inside her. "It's the wrong time of the month. I should be fine," she pleaded, not prepared to wait another second.

"No," he said bluntly.

There was no question in her mind that he wanted her... badly. But as her head cleared, she realized that Devlyn was not prepared to take even the slightest chance of fathering a child.

It made sense. It was the responsible, moral thing to consider. But what sobered Gillian was that moments ago *she* was beyond coherent reasoning. Devlyn had been able to step back.

Which meant she was in more trouble than she realized.

Devlyn shuddered, waves of heat raking his body painfully. The lack of a condom had stopped him from making a terrible mistake. He didn't deserve Gillian's generosity, her sweet, seductive body. Not when he knew his terrible sentence, the inescapable truth of what his past had made him.

His shaft nestled against Gillian's moist folds. The head pulsed and throbbed, desperate to push inward toward bliss. He could almost feel the tight squeeze of her slick passage.

His brain told him to get up, but the rest of him said a big *hell no!* He was right where he wanted to be...or at least close. Beneath him Gillian was soft, so soft. His entire weight rested on her. He smelled the warm fragrance of her skin, the unmistakable nuance of arousal, his and hers.

The dimly lit room was still and silent but for the sound of his harsh breathing and the ticktock of the antique mantel clock. He felt its measured cadence in his chest. He couldn't look at her, didn't want to see her confusion, possibly her hurt.

If he had ever wanted a woman more, he couldn't remember. But then again, it was not his style to get so carried away that he reached this impossible impasse.

Gillian lay beneath him, mute…unmoving.

Exerting an almost superhuman amount of will, he forced himself up and away from her, every group of nerves and muscles screaming in protest. By the time he made it to his feet, he was sweating.

She watched him dress. Which did nothing at all for his erection, even though he had moved some distance away. He felt her gaze like a caress.

Though he half expected her to follow his lead, she still lay naked on the sensuous fabric of the sofa. She had flipped to her stomach, and the vision of her long, narrow back curving out into her smooth, rounded ass made him ache with lust.

Licking her lips, she whispered an innocent question. "Do you want me to come to your bedroom?"

He turned away from her, his head crammed with images from the past, his and hers. What right did he have to take her, knowing that the relationship would have more to do with expedience than permanence? Gillian represented all that was good and decent about women. He had deep scars, wounds that compromised his ability to love a woman, any woman. Would his selfishness bring her pain, despite her protestations to the contrary?

Clearing his throat, he walked to the nearest shelf, blindly removing a volume. "Get dressed. Please."

After a moment of what seemed like stunned silence, he heard the rustling that indicated her compliance.

Her voice startled him when she spoke. "What now? Look at me, Devlyn. What now?"

He faced her across a distance of several feet. Her hair was tumbled, her eyes shadowed with uncertainty and regret.

As he glanced down at the book in his hands, he felt an insane urge to laugh. The volume he had picked at random was Dostoyevsky's *The Idiot*. Was fate trying to tell him something? Sadly though, if he remembered his high-school lessons correctly, the hero in that story was a good but naive man unable to navigate a not-so-admirable world.

Devlyn was neither naive, nor particularly good. But for Gillian, he would try. He dropped the book on the desk. "I promised not to push you, and I broke that promise. Perhaps it would be wise to take a step backward. Our involvement could complicate things."

Even in the dim light he saw her pale. Her expression was hard to read. But the dark eyes that gazed at him so solemnly judged him and found him wanting. "I can make decisions for myself," she said. "I don't need you to protect me, Devlyn...not even from yourself."

Her dignity in the face of his unforgivable about-face shamed him. "It's not you," he said.

Fury shot from her eyes. "Oh, please. Surely you can do better than that? I understand that you don't want to take a chance without birth control. I get that. What I can't fathom is why you're shutting me out."

Even now he wanted her so badly he was close to begging. For forgiveness, for comfort, for sexual release. But he didn't deserve her. Not by a long shot. So how could he justify playing fast and loose with her emotional well-being?

His timing sucked. He should have realized from the beginning that he was headed down a dead-end road.

For one agonizing moment he had a vision of Gillian with a chubby, dark-eyed baby at her breast. The image pained him so deeply his eyes grew damp. Yearning constricted his chest. All he had to do was treat her decently, and she might fall in love with him. He could be the man to give her babies.

But even as the temptation faced him, he shoved it away. He couldn't give her children. He wouldn't. Of all the women he'd ever wanted, Gillian was the one he knew, beyond any doubt, who would love with a mother's pure heart, the one who would cherish her babies and stand by them as they grew.

One day soon a man would walk into her life, a man who could give her what she wanted…what she needed. That man was not Devlyn.

Moving with the painful limbs of an old man, he walked slowly past her to the door. "Good night."

She didn't answer. And she didn't follow.

And that was when he truly understood what he was giving up.

Eleven

Gillian cried herself to sleep, loathing the fact that Devlyn had reduced her to an emotional cliché. All night she slept in fits and starts, waking to find herself in a strange bed, and then reliving over and over the humiliating scene in the library.

He'd ruined it for her…that wonderful room. Never again would she be able to set foot inside it. Not without remembering the look on his face. Did he think she was trying to trap him somehow? Surely not. He had made his position very clear. Only a madwoman would believe she had the power to change him.

When the alarm went off just after dawn, she lay in bed, trying to find the courage to face the day. She didn't have the luxury of flouncing out of the house in a huff. The income from this job was not mad money, it was her livelihood…at least for now. If she was lucky, some teacher in the region would go on maternity leave at Christmas, and Gillian might get to finish out the year. And perhaps next fall things might be better.

None of that helped her now.

At eight on the nose, a polite maid brought coffee and scones along with juice and assorted jams. Gillian thanked her, uncomfortably aware that the young woman no doubt knew and worked with Doreen. It shouldn't matter, perhaps, but it did.

After devouring the lovely breakfast, Gillian dressed in a professional but understated outfit. A jacket and midcalf-length skirt, dark camel, with a silk blouse in a pumpkin-and-gold paisley print. Low-heeled, dressy boots in a neutral color finished what she now thought of as armor.

When she was ready, she sat at the lovely mirrored vanity and looked at herself objectively. The woman staring back at her was neatly turned out, but unexceptional. Brown hair, brown eyes, a small gap between her front teeth because her mom had not been able to afford braces.

Her mouth was perhaps her best feature, nicely shaped and usually smiling. The rest of her was ordinary. Like millions of other females in the world, she was not model material, but neither would her face scare children. And that was okay. She'd never yearned to be a beauty queen…except for once in seventh grade when she'd had a crush on a boy two years older than she was.

When she'd had the temerity to profess her undying devotion, he'd looked at her chest and told her that boys liked boobs.

The experience had been both heartbreaking and instructive. From then on out, she'd set her sights on more suitable romantic liaisons. Until now…

Running a brush through her hair, she made the mistake of thinking about Devlyn doing the same thing with a firm but gentle touch on the night of her accident. It would be easier if she didn't like him so well…if she could write him off as an insensitive jerk.

Glancing at her watch, she jumped up with a groan. The next few hours would require every bit of maturity and composure she possessed. She would *not* allow him to see how much last night's aborted encounter had upset her. He'd made his decision. As far as anyone was concerned, Gillian was working for the Wolff family, assisting them on a project. Nothing more.

As she stepped out into the hall, she hesitated. Devlyn had set a time for their meeting, but not dictated a place. Which forced her to search out the gentleman who oversaw *all* the staff and to inquire of him as to Devlyn's whereabouts.

The stuffy but efficient majordomo led her to the solarium, a lovely foliage-filled room with three glass walls that brought the brilliant sunshine and autumn panorama inside a warm and cozy enclosure.

Devlyn was there before her, a sheaf of architect's renderings spread out on a plain wooden table. Wearing dark slacks and a long-sleeve oxford cloth shirt with the sleeves rolled up, he looked casual, but professional. Gillian forced herself to walk toward him and perch a hip on one of the stools that flanked the work surface. "Is this the school?" *Stupid, Gillian. What else would he be showing you?*

He lifted his head, his eyes searching her face. "Good morning. How did you sleep?"

"Probably better than you." She winced inwardly. Drawing attention to their short-lived lovemaking wasn't productive…not at all.

His gaze was bland, as if he hadn't understood her sarcastic comment. But she could swear she saw his lips twitch with silent humor. "Take a look," he said. "See what you think."

She was forced to lean over the table, uneasily aware that he was far too close given the way things had ended the night before. She could smell his aftershave. The brush of his arm against hers made her shiver.

Marshaling all her concentration, she glanced down at the drawings of the new school. It was an impressive layout and far larger than she had expected. Though her brain didn't necessarily work in such a fashion, she tried to visualize what it would all look like when it was finished.

Devlyn tapped a corner of the paper with a pencil. "Well, what do you think?"

"It's beautiful, of course."

"But?"

"But what?"

He sighed. "I hired you to give us direction. You're a teacher. You've been in the trenches on a daily basis. Tell me what's missing…what needs to be changed."

Devlyn was right. Her expertise was what he had hired her to contribute. She nibbled her bottom lip. "Well…"

"Don't be bashful. I need the truth."

"In that case, I'd flip these two wings." She pointed to a section of the blueprints. "The low commodes are for the kindergartners, but you have them situated as the farthest grade from the lunchroom."

Devlyn nodded, his sharp gaze already assessing, dissecting. "What else?"

"If money is not an issue, it would be great to have a portico over the front entrance, so that on rainy days car riders could be loaded in the dry."

"What about the buses?"

"Generally they come to the opposite side of the school. But since you'll have at least five or six loading all at once, the best you can do is park them 'nose in' and make the overhang extend past the door of the bus."

She could almost see the wheels turning in his brain.

Devlyn erased a mark and jotted a note. "Next?"

"This is a sort of selfish request, but I don't see a teachers' lounge. Elementary faculty members seldom have time to use one, but it's nice to know it's there. You'd want enough room for several couches, a refrigerator, a microwave…and a couple of lunch tables."

"Would two tables be enough?"

"Yes. They'll be rotating in and out…and probably with only twenty-five or thirty minutes to eat. Less than that once they drop the kids off in the lunchroom."

Devlyn looked shocked. "Good lord. Are you telling me that public-school teachers don't get the traditional hour for lunch?"

Gillian laughed out loud. "What a lovely idea, but no. Who do you think would watch the classes?"

"I don't know." He shrugged. "Monitor people, maybe."

"If you can work that out, you'll have potential employees lining up in droves."

They studied the plans for another half hour, Devlyn firing insightful questions at her, and Gillian offering suggestions based on her experience. But suddenly, they both fell silent.

She moved unobtrusively to the right, trying to put space between them. Even in the midst of a business discussion, she was far too aware of him. But what he was thinking was a mystery.

He glanced at his watch. "I want to show you the property. But no helicopters this time," he said hastily.

"Good to know. Otherwise I would have been forced to resign on the spot."

"What do you do when you fly?"

He seemed genuinely curious. So she was stymied as to how to explain.

"I've never been in an airplane, Devlyn. So it hasn't been as issue."

"That's terrible," he said. "Can't your doctor give you something for the vertigo?"

"It's not a question of medication."

"Then what? Is it that you can't overcome the phobia?"

She looked down at the plans, anything to avoid his gaze. Embarrassment flushed her throat and heated her cheeks. "It's the money, Devlyn. My father was a carpenter. My mother is a housekeeper. I barely made it through school on scholarships and a variety of minimum-wage jobs. I've never had the opportunity to fly."

He was stunned. And as embarrassed as she was. Clearly, to a Wolff, it was difficult to imagine a life where remaining earthbound was the norm. "I apologize," he said stiffly. "I'm usually not so obtuse."

"I'm not offended. And truthfully, I'd love to travel someday. When I have the opportunity."

She could see him struggle. To be honest, she had wondered if the reason he was reluctant to follow through with a physical relationship was that he recognized the differences in their circumstances. Perhaps he imagined that she would expect expensive gifts…or even worse, thought that she would try to extract money from him somehow.

The incident when he was eighteen surely impacted his ability to trust. Especially when it came to women and his wealth. No matter how she and Devlyn tried to ignore it, there was a definite class difference. She was Cinderella to his Prince Charming. Though she wasn't the one employed by the Wolff family in a service capacity—her mother was— the stigma remained, at least in Gillian's mind.

Devlyn rolled up the plans and slid them into a large tube. "The architect is meeting us at the property in half an hour. I'll join you in the front foyer in ten minutes."

Gillian scrambled after him, but he had already disappeared, swallowed up by the enormous house. She darted to her bedroom, grabbed her purse and a notebook and spent her final two minutes trying to remember the most direct route to the castle's entrance.

It wasn't a castle, not really, but it definitely qualified as more than a mere house. Devlyn beat her to the rendezvous point, his gaze moody as he cooled his heels.

"Sorry," she said. "I'm ready."

Someone had brought the car around. She'd hoped to make the trip in one of the roomy SUVs, a vehicle with plenty of interior space. Instead, Devlyn had chosen to take the Aston Martin again. She slid into the low, comfy seat and tried to ignore the fact that his hard, masculine thigh was mere inches away from hers. He was a big man. But the car suited him somehow.

With a screech of gravel, they swung out of the drive and onto the long road that twisted and turned for a good two miles before reaching the highway below. The hands that gripped the steering wheel were tanned and lightly dusted with black hair. Remembering the image of those masculine fingers, dark against her fair skin, caused Gillian's breath to hitch. She shifted nervously, feeling the interior shrink even more.

Staring out the window, she searched for something to say. "May I ask you a personal question?"

He shot her a sideways glance. "I suppose."

"Was there a woman sometime in the past who tried to sue you for paternity?"

His jaw was rigid, the cords in his neck standing out. "No. What gave you that idea?"

Regretting her impulsive inquiry, she squirmed. His tone warned her to step carefully. "It's the baby thing. You're so adamant. It made me wonder."

The sunny morning had changed without warning, heavy cloud cover rolling in from the west. "I've never let any woman have the power to put me in that position. So it hasn't been an issue."

He wasn't going to give her anything more than that. The silence lengthened. It was almost a relief when heavy drops of rain began to pelt the windshield. The noisy deluge masked Gillian's discomfort. How could she ever understand Devlyn if he stonewalled her anytime a personal topic was broached? On the surface, he was an extrovert…charming, affable, a social animal.

But beneath the charismatic persona ran a vein of dark, turbulent emotion.

She told herself it didn't matter. Devlyn needed her skills as a professional educator. Everything else would have to be pushed aside if this arrangement was going to work. But she didn't know how to keep herself from falling for him.

The whole idea behind the new school was that it be built very close to the tiny community of Burton. Consequently, it didn't take long to reach the parcel of land the Wolffs had already acquired. A silver Porsche was parked on the side of the road when they arrived.

Devlyn reached across Gillian's lap and pulled a fold-up umbrella out of the glove box. "Here," he said. "Do you want a rain jacket? I think I have one in the trunk."

His face was so close to hers she could have leaned forward a few inches and kissed him. She licked her lips. "No. It's not really cold. I'll be fine."

The car windows had fogged up almost instantly when he cut the engine. Devlyn stared at her, his eyes stormy. The look in them was unmistakable. He wanted her. "Gillian…I…"

She put her hand over his mouth, surprised at her daring. "You don't owe me any explanations, Devlyn. And just so we're clear on this, I'm a big girl. I'm not looking for a husband this month…or even this year. So you're in no danger.

I've done enough thinking. When you want me, all you have to do is ask."

Sitting back in her seat, she glanced out the window. "He's waiting for us. The architect."

Devlyn cursed. "Let him wait."

Slowly, as if trying to draw out the pleasure, he slid a hand beneath her hair, cupping her neck and dragging her across the console. "My leaving last night had nothing to do with not wanting you." His lips were cool but firm. His mouth moved against hers as if he had never kissed a woman. The very innocence of the caress made her crazy.

"Forget last night," she muttered, trying to breathe. "All I care about is today." Tangling her fingers in his thick, soft hair, she kissed him back.

Twelve

It wasn't in Devlyn's nature to be indecisive. Second-guessing decisions—or hesitating in the heat of the moment—meant losing out in the business world. His utter confidence and knack for innovative leadership were the reasons his father and uncle had chosen him to pilot the enormous behemoth that was Wolff Enterprises.

If they could see the current state of his brain, they'd have him committed.

Beneath his hands, Gillian's skin and hair were soft. Her scent, light and floral, soothed him even as it aroused him. "I don't know what to do with you." He heard the raggedness in his voice, recognized his own utter confusion.

She pulled away, smoothing her hair. "We have someone waiting for us," she said, not meeting his eyes.

He sensed her vulnerability. Did she think he was playing some kind of sexual power game? She'd be shocked if she knew that he was as conflicted as she was.

"Fine. Let's go. But we're not done with this."

Before he could come around and help her, Gillian was out of the car with the umbrella over her head. The rain had eased to a gentle drizzle. She walked by his side as they approached the man who awaited them.

Sam Ely was tall, rangy and rich. Maybe not by Wolff standards, but still well-heeled enough to draw the attention of every available woman in Charlottesville. He'd started his own architectural firm at twenty-five and now ran a multimillion-dollar business.

Sam smiled at Gillian with a lazy grin. "Sam Ely." He stretched out his hand. "You must be our new *expert*."

Devlyn watched, disquieted, as Gillian shook the architect's hand. "It's wonderful to meet you," she said. "Devlyn told me you're doing this project for half your normal fee. As a Burton native, I have to tell you how grateful I am."

Sam shrugged, a bashful *aw shucks* expression on his angular features. "I'm a sucker for little kids…what can I say? I'm honorary uncle to several of my fraternity brothers' kids…a dozen unofficial nieces and nephews already. And if my sweet grandma has her way, I won't be far behind in the procreation department."

Gillian laughed. "What does that mean?"

Sam took her elbow as they walked up a steep rise, leaving Devlyn to trail in their wake. "She's been setting me up with eligible women since the day I turned twenty-one. So far nothing has stuck, but any day now…"

"Is there someone special?"

He put an arm around her waist as she stumbled. "Take it easy. No…I'm still playing the field, but if I wait too long all the good ones will be taken."

The rain had stopped. Gillian lowered her umbrella and folded it up. "Somehow I doubt that will be a problem."

Devlyn snorted beneath his breath and wondered sourly if

Sam's slow Southern drawl was an affectation used to impress the ladies. Perhaps Devlyn should have thought twice about introducing Gillian at this stage in the game. He touched her shoulder, drawing her attention to the field ahead. "The stakes indicate the corners of the building. What do you think?"

The piece of property sat atop a small, flat-topped hill. Grading had not been a problem. The old farmer from whom they'd bought the land had plowed and planted this acreage for fifty years. There was plenty of room for the planned school, and even space for expansion one day, if needed.

Devlyn liked the idea that this verdant, grassy space would still be growing things…albeit children instead of corn and carrots. Gillian hadn't answered him. He turned and saw that her eyes were tear-filled.

"Thank you, Devlyn," she said, her words choked with emotion. "You're doing a very wonderful thing." She caught him completely off guard by hugging him tightly, her head tucked momentarily against his chest.

Over her shoulder his eyes met Sam's. The other man shrugged and smiled ruefully as if to say, *lucky guy.*

Devlyn allowed himself one quick squeeze and eased out of her grasp. He wasn't accustomed to indulging in personal moments during a business encounter. But then again, Gillian was teaching him new things about himself every day. The level of the regret he experienced in having to let her go was staggering.

Summoning his scattered brain cells, he motioned to the architect. "Let's walk room to room and I'll tell you how we want to tweak the design."

Gillian lingered behind the two men, turning in a circle to take in the view. Behind and above her, Wolff Castle sat somewhere atop its eagle perch, hidden from view by the forest that surrounded it. To the north, the Shenandoah Valley stretched for miles. Though the view today was shrouded in mist, she could visualize the panorama.

The school would be a showplace. She had seen the many windows in the drawings. Boys and girls of all ages would sneak peeks out of them in between assignments, dreaming of weekends and summers when they could run wild and free. This lush, remote, out-of-the-way spot was a great place to grow up.

Environmentally up-to-date, the school would generate much of its own electricity with solar panels and a wind turbine. Gillian had noticed a science lab in the plans, no doubt intended to be outfitted with sophisticated equipment. It warmed her heart to know that Burton's children, though from limited means, would have the opportunity and access to train for interesting careers.

The two men finished their circuit of the perimeter and returned to where she stood. Sam swept his arm in an arc. "I know it doesn't look like much yet, but I think you'll be impressed."

"I already am." Gillian glanced at Devlyn. "And I feel lucky to be part of such an exciting project."

Sam eyed Gillian. "How about I take you to lunch and I'll go over the blueprints with you…show you all the things I'm hoping to incorporate into the plans as we fine-tune them. You're welcome, too, Devlyn…of course."

Devlyn's handsome face darkened. "Not necessary. Gillian and I went over everything this morning."

Gillian wasn't stupid. Devlyn was staking a claim. Which made no sense at all, since he apparently didn't want to pursue a relationship with her. His arrogance was patronizing and irritating. She gave Sam a big smile. "I'd still love to hear your ideas in more detail," she said. She shot Devlyn a cool gaze. "I'm sure you have lots of important work to do for Wolff Enterprises, right? You won't miss me at all."

Sam swooped in smoothly to close the deal. "I'd be happy to drive Gillian up the mountain when we're done."

Devlyn smiled genially. "I hate to break up the party, but I really need Gillian this afternoon. Part of what we've hired her to do is deal with paperwork...and there's a mountain of it. Sorry, Sam. Maybe the three of us can get together another time."

Sam took his dismissal with good grace. "Too bad. But I'll take a rain check." After shaking both Gillian's hand and Devlyn's, he strode back to his car, got in and disappeared down the road.

Gillian was so mad her chest was tight. "That was the most appalling show of chest-beating I've seen in a long time. How dare you bully me like that? And in front of such a nice man."

Devlyn narrowed his eyes. "I did not bully you. I merely pointed out that we're not paying you to have long lunches with guys you've just met. You're my employee. If you want to date handsome architects, you can do it on your own time. And for your information, the jury's still out on whether or not Sam Ely is a nice guy. He has a reputation for enjoying the ladies."

"You're the last person I'd take dating advice from."

"I thought it was a business lunch. Now you're *dating* the man?"

She got up in his face. "Don't twist my words."

"Don't try to make me jealous." His yell echoed across the open space.

Gillian's jaw dropped. "I wasn't..." But was she lying to herself? Had she seen Sam as an easy shot at Devlyn?

He groaned, taking her by the hand and dragging her along behind him. "I want to show you something."

It petrified her how much she enjoyed holding hands with Devlyn Wolff. Such a simple thing, and yet so powerful.

"Slow down," she said. "The grass is all wet. I don't want to break my ankle."

He relented only slightly. She was breathless by the time they reached the back of the property. The fall of the land was not as steep on this side, and the grassy field gave way to a grove of hardwood trees. The vibrantly colored leaves overhead and underfoot—combined with the foggy, misty day—created a mystical place of beauty.

Devlyn halted eventually beside a tiny, wet-weather stream. He released her hand and squatted to remove a clump of leaves from a formation of smooth, moss-covered rocks.

"What is it?" she asked.

He cupped his hands, filling them with clear liquid and standing to face her. "Spring water. From a subterranean source. As clean and pure as the first day it was created. Taste."

He held it out, unsmiling. Gillian had the odd notion that they were enacting some kind of primitive ritual. She bent her head and sipped from his curved palms. The water was cold and tart, making her throat sting at the same time that it quenched her thirst.

Inevitably, her lips brushed his skin. The intimacy of his offering tapped something deep inside her. A sensual yearning to give herself to this man.

She took a second drink and lifted her head. "Thank you," she whispered, not daring to break the protective layer of quiet that cocooned them.

Before he could squat on his haunches for a second time and drink for himself, she crouched, giving not a thought to her nice outfit. Hands trembling, she gathered water, rose and offered it to him. "For you," she said, mentally urging him to let go of whatever chains held him back.

For long seconds she thought he was going to refuse. Giving her a dark, reluctant stare, he dipped his head and sucked up a great mouthful of spring water. His teeth grazed the sensitive pad beneath her thumb. The feel of his lips on her cold skin turned her inside out.

She wanted him dreadfully, and yet she knew the danger. Was she totally naive to think she could play with fire and walk away unscathed?

Water dripped from her hands when he thrust his tongue between her fingers, one at a time. Her knees literally went weak. "Devlyn…"

"Gillian." He mocked her gently.

"I can't do this on-again, off-again thing. It hurts too much. I don't expect you to commit to anything beyond this moment, but I have to know you need me as much as I need you."

"I don't," he said flatly, gathering her into his arms. "I need you more."

The last word was muffled as he moved his mouth over hers. Every time they were together she learned something new about him. Today it was the taste of kisses that combined remorse with promises. First gentle, then demanding, he staked a claim.

His tongue probed between her teeth, tangling with hers. She heard him moan. The sound of his hunger shuddered through her like hot honey. They were pressed so closely together that his heartbeat mingled with hers. His sex, eager and ready, pushed urgently against her flat belly.

What they were doing was wild, impractical, without reason. They had no blanket, nothing to cover the damp ground. And although it was not especially cold, getting naked might be another story.

"Devlyn?" She winnowed her fingers through his thick hair as he suckled a sensitive spot behind her ear.

He had either gone deaf or he was choosing to ignore her. But last night's awkward parting had made her cautious. Self-preservation was a strong instinct.

"Devlyn." She said his name a second time, more urgently. "What are you doing?"

He lifted his head for a moment, eyes glittering, cheekbones ruddy with arousal. "I'm tasting you." Beneath her jacket he stroked his hands over the slick fabric of her blouse.

Heat blossomed every place his hands touched. Running the tip of her tongue along his jawline to return the favor, she sighed. "I get that. But what about birth control?"

He went still, his expression tense. "Hell." Almost simultaneously, jubilation lit his face. "I have one," he croaked. "A condom. In my wallet." He released her and stepped back, at the same time extracting from his billfold what they needed and tucking it into his shirt pocket.

He grimaced. "You make me lose sight of everything. When I touch you, I burn. I never intended our first time to be in an October forest. But I don't think I can wait another minute to have you."

"You don't sound very happy about it," she muttered… though having a man speak as if he would die if he didn't have her was damned effective foreplay.

"Happy doesn't enter into it. You walked back into my life and it was as if I'd been struck by lightning. I can't explain it. And no…it's not the path I would have chosen. You deserve a man far better than I am. But I can't seem to resist you. If you feel for me even a fraction of what I do for you, I need you now."

"Here? Really?" She glanced around them as if a bed might magically appear.

"Trust me, Gillian. There are ways."

She had never seen such a look on a man's face. It thrilled and scared and aroused her in equal parts. The adult Devlyn was essentially a stranger to her, a man she had met less than forty-eight hours ago. Nothing about the situation was prudent or wise. But after last night, she couldn't deny him anything…didn't want to.

She had lived a lifetime of caution. But today was a new adventure. "Okay, then," she said. "Show me how."

Thirteen

Devlyn could barely hear her quiet response over the roaring in his head. He had plunged headfirst over a waterfall, tumbling wildly out of control. Was he really going to do this? Not only decide to make love to Gillian, but here? Now?

For a grown man, he was ridiculously confounded by their complicated circumstances and the lack of privacy. Gillian's mother's house was out for obvious reasons. And there were too many watchful eyes at the castle. Plus the fact that Gillian was uncomfortable being entertained there as a guest while her mother was an employee.

A Wolff, any Wolff, was too well-known to check into a local motel unnoticed. So here they were…

She stood watching him with those big, soft brown eyes. Vulnerable and brave, she wore her femininity gracefully. Too unsure of herself to take the lead, but not entirely convinced he would be good to her. That he could witness her hesitance shamed him. A woman deserved security in her lovers, a knowledge that coupling meant more than cheap sex.

If he could only express to her what he felt, the driving urge to possess her, to mark her, maybe then she would realize that this was no testosterone-driven whim.

But he couldn't explain her appeal to himself, much less to her.

She wrapped her arms around her waist.

"Are you too cold?" he asked, wincing as he heard the words. He sounded like a sixteen-year-old hoping to score behind the football stadium.

"I won't be," she said. "Not if you're holding me."

Glancing around them, he spotted a large tree stump, recently cut. The surface was rough, but mostly dry, protected in part by the canopy overhead. It would do. He picked her up, surprising a gasp from soft, pink lips. "Have you ever made love outdoors?"

She clung to him, arms around his neck. "Never."

"This will be a first for me, too." Her slender body, though not petite, was a negligible weight. He looked down at her, unsmiling, feeling twin currents of lust and tenderness converge in his chest. "We don't have to do this. I can wait. Probably." She felt so damned good in his arms...almost as if she belonged there.

Gillian laughed softly, the sexy sound making the hair on the back of his neck rise. "What would your employees in Atlanta say if they could see you now?"

He snorted. "They'd probably think I'd lost my mind. Kieran, my cousin, is the one who has no problem with sleeping on the ground and eating grubworms for breakfast. I'm more of a five-star hotel guy...soft sheets...a good bottle of wine. A beautiful woman."

"So you're zero for three and you still want to have sex with me?"

He stood her on the stump and put his hands on her hips to steady her. Looking up into the face of the woman who haunted his dreams at night, he was pained by the lack of confidence she exhibited in her desirability. His fingers dug into her flanks, itching to touch bare skin. "Don't tell me you're not beautiful," he said. "I'm the judge, and I happen to be pretty damned turned on right now in case you hadn't noticed."

"Men are like that." She gnawed her lower lip, her hands fluttering at her sides. It would take more than words to convince her.

He lifted the hem of her skirt and slid his hands up her thighs. "Pick up your foot," he commanded.

She was wearing sexy ankle-high boots with—thank God—no panty hose. Her skin was cool, but not particularly chilled. It was almost as soft as her blouse. He rubbed her thighs lightly, warming them with the friction of his caress.

Gently, teasingly, he curled his fingers in the waistband of her underwear and dragged it ever so slowly over her hips and down her legs. Gillian's eyelids fluttered shut, her lips parted. Observing nothing in her stance to indicate disagreement, he brought the silken scrap of nothing to her ankles.

Holy hell. No sexy movie star had ever looked as deliberately alluring. His hands shook and his shaft hardened to stone. "Step out of them, Gillian." His voice was firm.

She put her hands on his shoulders and obeyed, lifting one foot at a time. He tucked the undies in his hip pocket, put his hands on her waist and lifted her effortlessly, depositing her onto the ground.

Unzipping his trousers he freed himself from the knit boxers that threatened to cut off the blood flow to the part of his body that demanded attention.

"Touch me, Gillian." The guttural words were both command and plea.

She stared at him…first skimming her gaze over his face…then assessing his straining erection. Licking her lips like someone anticipating a treat, she took him in her hands and warmed his length. He could have told her it was unnecessary. The skin that was pulled so tightly over firm flesh throbbed and burned from the inside out. He braced his legs and dug his hands into her hair.

Every brush of her delicate fingertips marked him indelibly. Beneath her touch, his shaft leaped eagerly, aching to find release. His brain held sway...barely. He was determined to draw this out, to give Gillian the full measure of his attention, his hunger, his absolute focus.

But even a strong man had his limits. And Gillian brought him to the edge far too rapidly. Gently, he removed her hands and stepped away. Fumbling in his pocket, he located the single condom, ripped it open and held it out with a raised eyebrow.

She was bashful, clearly. He swallowed hard, his throat dry. "Please," he said. "I want you to." Her movements were sweetly clumsy as she did her best to position the latex over the head of his penis. A couple of false starts tested his patience. Finally, she managed to cover him from base to tip.

He sat down on the stump and held up his arms. "Come here, honey. Let me love you."

In her face he saw the battle between shock and excitement. Lucky for him, the latter won. She lifted her skirt and straddled his legs. He almost had an orgasm right then.

Finding her bare butt beneath her skirt, his hands guided her descent. "Easy, baby. Slowly. Do it slowly."

Her hands hovered and finally found a resting place on his shoulders. Gradually, a bit at a time, she sheathed him in her hot, moist passage. Groaning, barely coherent, Devlyn decided to shut up and let Gillian take the lead for the moment. The feel of her lithe body welcoming him was indescribable. She was silent, concentrating on the joining of their flesh. Soft and hard, male and female, as elemental as time itself.

When she had him fully seated, the head of his shaft nudging the entrance to her womb, she exhaled as if she had been holding her breath. "Oh, lordy…"

Gillian winced inwardly, embarrassed to let him see that she was in way over her head. Her few sexual experiences in the past bore no resemblance at all to what was happening at this very moment in a surprisingly sensitive spot deep within her sex.

Devlyn had his eyes closed, his head canted backward as he surged into her, flexing his hips. The strength hidden beneath his conservative clothing was astounding. He had carried her with ease. Even now, he thrust with power, filling her repeatedly.

She was on top, but that was where any semblance of domination on her part ended. Like a maestro, he played her body, slowly when it suited him…then hard and fast, making them both cry out.

His arms went around her waist, dragging her closer. The chill of the air did nothing to cool them. Skin hot and damp, he made love to her tirelessly. At moments when it was clear she was near the edge, he eased back on the rhythm, calming her frantic movements, slowing the pace.

Her skirt was rucked up to her waist, her half-naked body on display. She had never been an exhibitionist, but at the moment, modesty was the farthest thing from her mind. Desperately, she wanted to feel his mouth on her breasts, his hands on the bare skin of her back. But that would involve stopping, and she couldn't find the words to say what she felt.

Inside her, he felt enormous. She loved the sense of connection, the intimacy of their fevered coupling, the sensation of him filling her, claiming her.

Her breath caught as the inevitable climax sneaked up and

sent her reeling. "Devlyn…" Her shocked cry startled a trio of birds, who darted off into the treetops.

He held her close while she rode out the last fluttering tremors of her release. Head on his shoulder, she struggled to breathe. "I'm sorry," she muttered. "You haven't…"

He played with her hair, his big frame shuddering with un-appeased arousal. "I will. Not to worry. Give me your mouth."

It never occurred to her to protest. Their lips met, tasted, slid apart. A tiny buzz of remembered pleasure regenerated her arousal. Something about the fog and the sylvan glade enhanced her pleasure…a dreamy, unfocused, self-satisfied urge to wallow in Devlyn's passionate persuasion.

He nipped her bottom lip with his teeth. "You're going to come again."

The certainty in his ragged voice made moisture bloom in secret places she'd thought well satisfied already. *If you say so…* So intense was the vein of joy, she would have agreed to most anything.

"God," he groaned. "Where's a bed when you need one?"

She licked the whorl of his ear. "I can lie on the ground. It won't matter."

"It matters to me. You deserve to be cherished." He chuckled raggedly, despite his obvious urgency. "I think I may have lost my mind."

Wiggling her hips experimentally, she imagined his big, masculine body on top of hers. The image brought her to the edge a second time. Panting, impatient, she ripped at the buttons on his shirt. "Put this on the ground," she pleaded. "I want to feel you on top of me."

His face flushed dark red. Indecision painted his features. "Are you sure?"

"Yes, Devlyn. Yes."

Still buried inside her, he wriggled out of the sleeves. She undid the last button and tossed the shirt on the leaf-covered ground. "I'll go first," she said, already lifting herself from him.

His fingers dug into her hips. "Don't. Don't move."

She obeyed.

He cursed, the words choked and broken. And then it was too late. With a shout, he exploded…hard…hips pistoning wildly as he thrust, his shaft rubbing intimately at her inner flesh that was already too sensitive.

Stunned, she whimpered a sobbing cry. "Oh, oh, oh…" The second peak was more powerful than the first. Wrapped in his fierce embrace, she felt everything she thought she knew about herself incinerate…flare brightly…and fade away.

What was left behind in the aftermath was an odd sense of peace. For so long she had assumed she knew what she wanted out of life. A dependable, kind mate, a handful of children, security.

But what she had discovered instead was that she had a wild, self-destructive streak. Devlyn was dangerous…in so many ways. He was a lone Wolff, a sociable animal whose affability masked a complicated personality with enough layers to stymie a psychotherapist.

She couldn't discern his secrets, and she didn't really have the right to ask. Whatever the nature of the relationship they found themselves embroiled in, it surely didn't include the kind of permanence that merited shared confidences.

It was sex.

For some unfathomable reason, Devlyn wanted her. It wouldn't last. She knew that. But for better or for worse, she wanted him, too.

Seconds passed, perhaps entire minutes. Gradually their breathing returned to normal. And almost simultaneously Gillian felt awkwardness roll over her in a suffocating wave.

She wanted to stand up, but she wasn't sure her legs would

support her. Devlyn seemed in no hurry to move. So her hands roved with a will of their own over the smooth, taut skin of his back. Muscles flexed beneath her touch. The part of her that was feminine, vulnerable, responded to his latent power. In prehistoric times he would have been the kind of man who kept danger at bay, protecting the weak and the defenseless.

Gillian was a fully evolved woman. She had a career. Or at least she would have one again sometime. She knew how to change a tire. Was not averse to killing the occasional mouse. Balanced her own checkbook, planned for the future.

She didn't *need* a man to shield her from the world. But despite all evidence to the contrary, she craved Devlyn's unspoken strength. His personality was so unlike her own. Though she was more of an introvert, her past was an open book. Ordinary. Boring.

His silence made her uneasy. Was she supposed to say something? Do something?

In the absence of conversation or even the unmistakable sounds of lovemaking, the woods teemed with sound…a whip-poor-will's call, the rustle of small creatures scurrying through the underbrush.

Devlyn's face was buried against the side of her neck. She almost imagined that his lips moved on her skin.

Did she want tenderness from him so badly that she was willing to manufacture emotion where there was none?

For the first time since they had walked into the glen, cold seeped into her veins, chilling her from the inside out. Goose bumps erupted in places she'd rather not contemplate. At the risk of committing a sexual faux pas, she stood shakily, allowing the connection, flesh to flesh, to be broken.

Hurriedly, she smoothed her skirt. She bent and picked up Devlyn's shirt, holding it out to him. "At least we didn't ruin it."

Was that supposed to be a self-conscious attempt at humor?

If it was, Devlyn ignored it. He stood and straightened his clothing, taking the wrinkled garment from her hand without comment and putting it on.

As she watched him adjust his boxers, tuck in his shirt and zip his slacks, her stomach curled in mortification. His movements were unhurried, matter-of-fact. He must have dealt with the condom when she looked away.

Gillian was a wreck. Last night she had been hurt by his rejection. Now she was satisfied physically, but as confused as ever.

Devlyn was cool as ice.

Fourteen

The last time Devlyn remembered feeling this level of sexual agitation was the night after he lost his virginity. It disturbed him that the old wound echoed in today's encounter. But it made sense in a way. He lusted after Gillian, but he felt sleazy for having taken her, despite her compliance. Last night he had managed to walk away. Today, he had failed. Guilt and sexuality made uneasy bedfellows.

Wincing inwardly, he found her underwear in his pocket and handed it over. Gillian's face was rosy with color, her gaze downcast. She took the bikini, bent at the waist and stepped gracefully into it, ignoring his attempt to steady her. His hand dropped to his side. Undoubtedly she expected him to say something. After all, they had just indulged in wild, uninhibited, reckless sex. Or by another definition, spontaneous combustion.

She adjusted the collar of her blouse and smoothed her hair. Those simple, elegant motions dared him to dishevel her again, though he was certain she didn't mean to convey that.

He cleared his throat. "Gillian?"

She looked up at him, her expression guarded. "Yes?"

"Oh, hell." Dragging her into his embrace, he gave her a hard, heated kiss before holding her at arm's length and staring into her eyes, willing her to understand. "I'm flying blind here, honey. You've knocked me six ways to Sunday."

Suspicion etched a tiny wrinkle between her brows. "You sleep with women all the time. Everyone knows that."

"You aren't a woman."

"Excuse me?" The frown disappeared when her brows rose toward her hairline.

Good God. "You're not a *normal* woman," he clarified.

Gillian struggled free, her chest heaving in a way that threatened to distract him again. "Are you *trying* to make me regret what just happened here?"

He ground his teeth. "You know what I mean. You're different. Special."

"As in mentally unbalanced?"

"Quit putting words in my mouth, damn it." Heat washed up his neck.

"Somebody needs to. If this is your idea of pillow talk, I'm amazed you ever have a second date."

"For a female who comes across as shy and polite, you're sure loosening up." He was bemused by his utter lack of savoir faire. He'd built a reputation both in the bedroom and the boardroom as a slick operator. Yet Gillian managed to disconcert him time after time.

Prim and proper on the outside, a hot, silver flame in his arms. She didn't look at all like a woman who had just been thoroughly— Even in his own mind, he had to censor his language. Gillian made him want to be a better man.

She sighed audibly. "Can we go home now?"

Her pallor disturbed him. "Are you okay?"

She shrugged. "I don't know what I am. But I won't stay

at the castle anymore. I'll do your job. Help with the school… but this…" She waved a hand at their unorthodox trysting place. "It's really a bad idea."

"Didn't seem that way a few minutes ago." She had grit. He had to give her that. In spite of her painfully evident embarrassment, she met his gaze head-on.

"Devlyn…" She stopped and exhaled an exasperated breath. "You know how appealing you are…charming, sexual, physically close to perfect…"

"Close?"

"Focus, big guy. You have all the cards. It isn't fair. I don't know why you're slumming with the housekeeper's daughter."

His temper fired. "I've never been accused of being a snob. And damn, but it must be exhausting carrying that chip on your shoulder. I *like* you. Is that so hard to believe?"

She bit her lip. "Truthfully? Yes."

"Are you really that unsure of yourself?"

"Not as a rule. But then again, the men I've been with… and I can count them on less than one hand…they were… well…*normal*."

His lips twitched. He saw the moment she realized what she had said. "That word must have multiple meanings," he drawled. Finally, she smiled, and the knot in his gut eased a bit.

"You are incorrigible."

"There you go again…using five-syllable teacher words. It makes me hot."

"Forgive me if I point out that you're what we call *easy*."

"And you're not easy at all. Where does that leave us?"

"As the woman who recently allowed you to lift my skirt and have your way with me, I haven't a clue."

"How would you feel about moving our relationship to private territory?"

She tilted her head, frowning slightly. "You'll have to give me more than that."

"I have to go back to Atlanta after a carnival fundraiser for the school. I'd like you to return with me to Georgia."

"Why?"

"Because I'd like a chance for us to be alone together. Really alone. With no one to interfere."

"And in the meantime?"

"You were the one screaming my name a little while ago. You tell me."

"God, you're smug." But she smiled as she said it, so he figured he was okay.

"Was that a yes?"

She lifted her chin, looking down her nose at him with that prissy, disapproving, narrow-eyed gaze that made him want to kiss her senseless. "I suppose I could be persuaded to go to Atlanta with you. But in the meantime…I'm conflicted. Maybe we should abstain. It's not really practical to sneak around outside, and the thought of your family walking in on the two of us in flagrante delicto gives me hives."

"I don't even know what the heck that means, but it sounds dirty, so I like it." Her suggestion wasn't entirely unreasonable, though it might be hard to pull off. Maybe he could wait until Atlanta. It would give him time to deal with his unanswered questions about his own culpability if he let things get too serious.

She kicked at a pile of leaves with the toe of her boot. "Don't play dumb with me, Devlyn Wolff. They don't put imbeciles in charge of worldwide corporations. Earning that MBA you've got tucked in your back pocket required a lot of brain power."

He shrugged. "I'm good at math. It's no big deal."

"Not from where I stand. Overseeing an organization like Wolff Enterprises requires a complex skill set. You act as if it's a walk in the park, but I know how hard you work. Just because you make it look easy, don't assume that people take you at face value. You're a financial genius. And I know your father and your uncle are very proud."

Her quiet praise affected him in ways he couldn't explain. Gillian was *real* and honest and thoughtful. Hearing her sincere compliments humbled him.

The serious turn in the conversation was unexpected and gratifying. But he had more carnal concerns on his mind. "So we're going to try to be platonic?"

He moved toward her, grinning when she backed up and almost fell over a root.

"Stay where you are." Her cheeks were flushed again.

He held up his hands. "I was only going to kiss you."

"Look where that got us last time."

Her quick glance at the abandoned stump was enough to make him hard. Again. She didn't protest when he pulled her arms around his neck. "Kiss me," he coaxed. They were plastered together, chest to chest, but fully clothed this time.

Gillian's lips met his. He tasted her smile, her yielding, her sweet, almost innocent trust.

She tipped back her head and gazed at him, eyes filled with feminine secrets. "Are you going to wine and dine me in the big city?"

"Among other things." He'd already taken her once like a wild man. Would it be entirely out of line to try again?

He was shocked as hell when she decided to play with his zipper. Her face, shielded by a fall of dark brown hair, was hidden from him as she whispered a tempting offer. "I've always heard that to go cold turkey on something, sex, for instance, you should overindulge before you begin to deny yourself."

"Hell, yes. Smart woman. I knew there were benefits to being the teacher's pet."

She found his rigid shaft and stroked it. "Is that what you think you are?"

Her long fingers curled around him and squeezed. He groaned. "Easy there, Gillian. Have mercy." He felt like it had been days since he'd taken her...not minutes.

She released him and stepped back. "You're right. Besides, everyone knows anticipation is half the fun. Tell me again. What day are we leaving?"

He bent at the waist, his brain mush. "The carnival is tomorrow night. We'll leave first thing Saturday," he croaked. Surely she didn't intend to leave him like this.

Her smile was sunny. "I accept your invitation. I'm going to head back to the car. I'll let you finish up here." She turned and took a step in the opposite direction.

"The hell you say." He was ninety-nine percent sure she was teasing. But that one percent scared the crap out of him. Snagging her wrist in an unbreakable hold, he dragged her back. "Not nice, Gillian. You're not going anywhere."

Huge, long-lashed chocolate eyes looked at him mischievously. "Is there a problem?"

He took her hand and placed it over his erection. "*You're* the problem," he said, realizing that he was dead serious. What was he going to do with her?

She cupped him in both hands, going up on tiptoe to kiss him gently. "Don't worry, Mr. Wolff. I'll take it from here."

Gillian barely even recognized herself. Sexual banter? Erotically teasing and taunting a man who far outstripped her in experience of almost every kind? What had possessed her?

As she played with Devlyn's impressive shaft, she acknowledged that the question was not *what,* but *who.* Devlyn. Her lover.

He was steel sheathed in silky warm skin. Moisture oozed from the head of his erection, signaling his readiness to take her again. Understanding the full measure of how much she wanted that to happen told her she was beyond turning back.

The journey had begun. The ship cast away from its moorings. The die was cast. Any cliché she could pick. Her only hope was to enjoy Devlyn while he was hers and do her best not to beg when he was done and ready to move on.

He would try not to hurt her. That much she knew for sure. But trying was not the same as succeeding. It would be up to her to protect her heart.

Even now, seeing him at a man's most vulnerable point, her instinct was to protect him, to make him happy. The naïveté in that goal should have shamed her. Did she really want to be one in a long line of faceless women who had warmed Devlyn's bed?

But as much as she needed to be with him in the most elemental way, she also had a painful urge to save him from himself. Something in his past hung as a millstone around his neck. She knew it. And though he had shared glimpses of the events that shaped him, there was something more, something darker.

The possibilities scared her. She didn't want to rip open old wounds and have him hate her for it. But perhaps fate had brought the two of them together for a reason.

As she rubbed him with a delicate touch, he put his hand over hers. "Harder," he pleaded. "Faster."

She wanted him inside her when he reached climax. But it was an impossible situation at best. While she and Devlyn had been concentrating on each other, light rain had sneaked back into their wooded glade. It dripped from leaves overhead, filling the air with the humid, pungent scent of decaying leaves.

As Devlyn trembled in her embrace, she saw the depth of his trust. He was completely open to her, unguarded, intimately exposed.

Something cracked inside her, a wall she had tried to keep

in place to protect her heart. But it was too late. Feelings rushed in like floodwaters swamping a breach. It would be so easy to love him…and yet so terribly unwise.

Swallowing the lump in her throat, she tried to separate her messy emotions from the sensual experience at hand. Pushing aside everything but the need to pleasure him, she did as he asked. Faster. Harder. Devlyn moaned. Without words, he had allowed the balance of power to shift momentarily.

His big body warmed her, hands clenched on her shoulders, legs braced like bulwarks against the storm. When she hit a sensitive spot, he quaked and sank his teeth into her earlobe.

The sharp sting of pain made her belly quiver with hunger. Twice she had climaxed, and yet she wanted him again. To prove to herself that she still had some sort of sexual backbone, she concentrated on Devlyn. Denying her own need demonstrated that she could walk away at any time. When the situation became untenable.

She was not a victim, nor a helpless, fragile female. Choosing to be with Devlyn was a rational, eyes-wide-open decision.

He kissed her temple, his breath hot on her cheek. "I'll finish." The words were barely audible, his breath wheezing raggedly.

Leaning into him, both of her hands trapped between their bodies, she circled the head of his erection and brushed the eye. Devlyn came with a muffled curse.

When it was over, the silence was absolute but for the beat of her heart in her ears, and the faint chatter of a squirrel in a nearby tree.

Fifteen

On the way back to the car, Devlyn held Gillian's hand. She had no way of knowing, and he sure as hell wouldn't tell her…but that last bit of insanity was something he had never wanted, nor requested from any woman, ever.

It was no secret that he liked being in the driver's seat. He could tell himself that the only reason he had allowed her to pleasure him was that there was no other suitable alternative. But in truth, he had craved her touch like an addict coming off a three-day bender.

Her fingers were cold in his. He tucked her into the car and turned on the heat. They were both wet and rumpled, and God knew, it would be a good idea if they could slip into the house and change without being seen. He'd be hard-pressed to explain why they had lingered outside at the school site when the weather deteriorated.

The fact that neither of them said a word as they made their way back up the mountain didn't bother him. One of the things he liked about Gillian was her innate calm, her quiet serenity. They had talked plenty back there. The important things were said. Gillian had committed to accompany him to Atlanta.

Like a kid anticipating Christmas, Saturday couldn't arrive quickly enough to suit Devlyn.

Unfortunately for both of them, slipping into the house unnoticed was not an option. The massive front doors of the castle were flung open wide, and a trio of young men took turns unloading suitcases from a chauffeur-driven limousine.

Gillian squirmed in her seat, trying futilely to smooth the wrinkles from her damp skirt. "What's going on?" she asked.

He pulled the car to one side of the sweeping courtyard and parked. "At a guess, I'd say my sister has arrived. She's in charge of the carnival."

"That would be Annalise, right? I remember her. I was terribly jealous of her clothes and her toys. Not a very nice thing to admit, but I was just a kid."

"Annalise always loved playing dress up. And nothing has really changed."

"Do you think anyone will notice if we walk around to the back of the house?"

Devlyn shook his head, grinning as he smoothed a tendril of hair from her flushed cheek. "That ship has sailed, Gillian. Our best bet is to brazen it out."

Her smile was wry. "I'm thinking you have more experience with that kind of behavior than I do."

He kissed her softly, closing his eyes for a split second as the taste of her filled him with contentment. "Then follow my lead."

Despite his assurances, the situation went downhill as they entered the impressive front foyer. Not only was Annalise there, but also Devlyn's father, his uncle and Gillian's mother. Doreen Carlyle was holding a dustcloth and a broom.

Beside him, Gillian stiffened.

Gradually, everyone froze when he and Gillian entered, conversation dwindling, and all eyes going to the unmistakable evidence that Devlyn and Gillian had been tramping through the woods. No one could possibly know what that outing included, but Gillian's bright red face wasn't helping matters.

Annalise launched herself at him, going in for a bear hug as was her custom. He kissed her cheek. "What ill wind blew you in?"

His tall, willowy sister smacked his cheek lightly. "Be nice. I hoped you'd be glad to see me."

She turned and smiled at Gillian. "And who might this be? I thought you kept all your glittery girlfriends in Atlanta."

Devlyn bristled. Annalise had a kind heart, but a smart mouth. His surge of protectiveness warned him he was navigating new waters, but he couldn't allow Gillian to be embarrassed any more than she already was. "This is Gillian Carlyle. She's working with me on the new school project. As an educational consultant."

Doreen stepped forward, her face an older, rounder version of her only child's. "Gillian's my daughter, Miss Annalise. You probably don't remember. It's been years since she was here on the mountain."

Annalise held out her hand. "Sorry, Ms. Carlyle. If you're working with my brother, you deserve my sympathies."

"Call me Gillian, please." Gillian shook hands with Annalise and then hugged her mother. "I'd love to stay and chat, but we got caught in the rain and I'm freezing. Excuse me."

Devlyn was forced to let her escape, doomed to run interference with his relatives. Doreen excused herself as well, but disappeared down a corridor opposite from the one where her daughter was changing clothes. Devlyn spent a blissful second imagining his lover naked before he was forced to direct his attention elsewhere.

He glanced at the accumulating pile of luggage. "Are you moving in permanently?"

Annalise shrugged. "I wasn't sure what the weather would be this weekend, so I had to come prepared."

Devlyn's father, Vincent, grinned at his only daughter. "Leave her alone. I'm still hoping that one day I can keep her here for good."

Annalise pecked his weathered cheek with a kiss. "I love you, Papa."

Victor spoke up, combing through a pile of mail on a silver salver. "What did Gillian think of the property?"

"She was impressed. Sam met us there and walked off the rooms, giving her an idea of the layout."

Annalise's cheerful grin dimmed. "Sam Ely? What is Satan's offspring up to these days?"

"I've never understood why the two of you hate each other so much. After all, you work in the same building." Devlyn wasn't blind to his sister's antipathy. He just didn't understand it.

She shrugged. "Personality conflict. He doesn't have one."

The two older men chortled. Devlyn grinned wryly. "Well, Gillian was sure taken with him. He tried to whisk her away for an intimate lunch, but I nixed that."

"Because you have your eye on her?" Annalise's gimlet stare almost made him squirm. Almost.

"Because we have paperwork to get through this afternoon," he said. "Those permits won't fill out themselves."

He didn't think she was fooled, but thankfully, she dropped it. A few minutes later, Devlyn managed to escape, as well.

After showering and changing into corduroy slacks and a cashmere V-neck sweater, he tapped lightly on the connecting door to Gillian's suite. After long, agonizing seconds, she opened it.

She was wearing an outfit similar to his, only her lilac cardigan and silky ivory camisole outlined pretty breasts. Breasts Devlyn had recently tasted. He leaned in the doorframe, not trusting himself to go anywhere near her bed. "Do you feel like getting some work done?"

"Of course."

He frowned when he looked past her and realized that her packed suitcase stood ready for departure.

Her soft lips were covered in light pink lip gloss. He saw the movement of her smooth throat when she swallowed.

"Running away, Gillian?"

His sarcasm made her frown. "I told you I wouldn't stay here."

"You don't trust me," he said flatly, disturbed by how much that hurt.

"I don't trust us," she said. "This afternoon I want you to go over the paperwork with me. I have my laptop at home. I'll work from there until Saturday."

"And you'll go with me?"

"I said I would."

The sexual energy that swirled between them was almost palpable. His fingertips dug into the doorframe, holding himself in place. "Less than forty-eight hours," he groaned. "I don't know if I'll make it."

She blushed prettier than any woman he had ever met. Not that many of his female acquaintances actually blushed. He tended to date sleek, predatory versions of himself.

"Won't your father think it's odd that you hired me and I'll be leaving so soon?"

"We can work on the project in Atlanta." He straightened. "May I come in?"

She hesitated, but the flare of need in her eyes matched

the burning hunger in his belly. "We're practicing abstinence, remember?"

He held up his hands. "Only a kiss. I promise."

Gillian nodded slowly. It was no use to pretend. She wanted him. And falling in love with him would be as easy as breathing. Certain heartbreak loomed ahead like a deadly reef. But she refused to look in that direction.

Devlyn reeled her in and bent his head to trace each side of her collarbone with his tongue. He smelled divine, a combination of shower soap and a faint hint of woodsy cologne. She wrapped her arms around his neck and flexed her fingers in the soft wool of his sweater.

He mumbled something into her neck.

"I can't hear you." She tilted her head to one side as he nibbled her throat.

"Lock your door. I'll be quick."

Her knees went weak and her panties grew damp. "No." As a negative, it lacked authority.

His hand slid over her silky chemise and toyed with a beaded nipple. "Please." Even through two layers of fabric, his touch was electric.

She never had a chance to answer. A loud knock at Devlyn's outer doorway was followed by his father's booming summons. "You decent, boy? Vic and I want to talk to you about the Mexico deal."

Devlyn dropped his head to her shoulder, cursing eloquently beneath his breath. "I love my father, I love my father, I love my father…"

She giggled despite her disappointment. "Go," she said softly, allowing herself one last stroke of his hair.

With obvious pained difficulty, he straightened. "Meet me in the main dining room in an hour. We'll spread everything out and go from there."

For some reason, his words gave Gillian an image of herself, nude, spread-eagled on the table as a feast for Devlyn Wolff. Her sweater was suddenly far too hot for the temperature of the room. "I'll be there," she croaked. She shoved him away. "Go."

By the time she met him at the appointed place, she had regained control of her senses. They managed to conduct an impersonal, professional discussion about each one of the many permits and forms required for the start of a new school.

Of course, it helped that at least four different doors opened off the dining room, meaning that privacy was nonexistent. Various employees whisked in and out, readying the room for the evening's upcoming family dinner.

The architect's plans had already been tentatively approved. Once Gillian's suggestions were implemented, one more draft would be submitted and the project would be one step closer to groundbreaking.

When they had sifted through every layer of red tape, Gillian straightened the mass of paper and tucked it into a folder. "I'll spend all day on these tomorrow," she said, conscious of listening ears. "I should be able to get a good start."

"But you'll be attending the carnival, right?"

"I don't really know anything about it."

Devlyn leaned a hip on the table, laughing when one of the older maids gave him a swat on the behind. "LaVonn has known me since I was in grade school." He kissed her wrinkled cheek.

The African-American woman, surely nearing retirement, grinned. "This one was a handful. Always stealing cookies out of the kitchen."

"I was a growing boy."

"You were a menace." With a chuckle, she disappeared toward the kitchen.

Gillian was touched and confused. Who was the real Devlyn Wolff? This easygoing charmer, or the man with dark shadows in his past?

He folded his arms over his chest, snapping his fingers. "Earth to Gillian. The carnival is tomorrow night. Several members of the community wanted to have an event where they could contribute by creating a sense of local ownership in the project. Annalise offered to coordinate everything. We'll have inflatables, games, food. And all the money raised will be grassroots donations."

"That's a lovely idea."

"I'll be taking a turn in the dunking booth. How's your throwing arm?"

"I played intramural softball for four years in college. You should be very afraid."

Again, that naughty spark leaped and quivered. She cleared her throat. "My mother gets off duty in thirty minutes. If we're done here, I'll ride back down the mountain with her."

"Stay for dinner." Devlyn's eyes were dark, his expression sober. "My cousins and their wives will all be here…and Annalise. It will be fun."

"I don't want to give anyone the wrong impression of our relationship," she whispered. Even to her own ears the words sounded prissy.

Devlyn stood and straightened, a shadow of hurt in his eyes. "They know you're working here. You'll still be on the clock. I'll expect you at seven sharp."

He left the room abruptly, leaving her to hover uncertainly. She felt the oddest notion that she had injured his feelings, but that was absurd.

She went in search of her mother and found her putting away cleaning supplies in a hall closet off the kitchen wing. Gillian blurted it out. "I've been invited to eat with the family this evening."

Doreen's hands stilled. Her eyes mirrored anxiety and reluctance. "Are you sure that's wise? It's only a job, baby. We don't belong here."

"I realize that, Mama. Don't worry. I know what I'm doing."

Doreen kissed her cheek, took a garment from a hook and slipped her arms into the ten-year-old raincoat. "You're a grown woman. You don't need my permission. But I want you to be careful."

Gillian hugged her mom, inhaling the familiar scent of dusting spray. "Thank you for being concerned. But I'll be okay. I promise."

Wandering back to her temporary suite, she decided to check one more time and make sure she had retrieved all her belongings. When she opened her bedroom door, Annalise Wolff sat in a chair, slim, elegant legs crossed, her gaze unapologetic. "We need to talk."

Sixteen

Gillian's belly clenched. She put the folder on the dresser and turned to face the woman whom she had envied for many years as an adolescent. "About what? Do you have some ideas for the school?" But that made no sense, because Annalise would have gone to Devlyn directly if she had input to offer.

"About the fact that you're falling for my brother."

"Don't be absurd," Gillian said calmly, her pulse racing with anxiety. "We're working together for a brief time, that's all."

"I saw the way you looked at him when you both walked into the house."

"You're imagining things. We only recently ran into each other. He didn't even remember me at first."

"But I'm sure you took care of *that*. You've known him for years, long enough to realize that my family protects its own. If you have an angle to play, I warn you…I will do anything to make sure my brother doesn't get railroaded. He has a noble but regrettable tendency to pick up misfits and strays. And you wouldn't be the first woman to have eyes for his bank balance."

Gillian's hands fisted at her sides. "Are you always this rude, or is it me?"

"Devlyn may look as if his life is smooth sailing, but he's had some tough things to deal with over the years."

"You all have," Gillian said quietly. Annalise's plain speaking was understandable. The Wolffs stuck together for the good of the clan. "You have nothing to fear from me," she said. "I swear. My relationship with Devlyn is strictly temporary."

Either business or pleasure…the statement held true for both.

Annalise stood, tall and proud, immeasurably sophisticated. "I notice you haven't denied loving him."

"Devlyn is an admirable man. And I'm happy to be working with him. That's all."

The other woman passed her on the way to the door. "I hope for your sake that you're telling the truth. Because Devlyn will never settle down to home and hearth."

"Not that it matters to me, but why are you so sure?"

Annalise's eyes held a hint of the pain that Gillian had witnessed more than once in Devlyn's. "I just know," she said flatly. "So consider yourself forewarned."

After that, Gillian was in no mood to participate in a Wolff family dinner, but Devlyn had given her no choice. His high-handed demand left her angry and confused. Why had he insisted on her presence? She showered and washed her hair before changing into a pair of black dress slacks and a crimson silk blouse. The flattering outfit bolstered her confidence. There was a good chance that the ensemble was not dressy enough for Wolff standards, but it was her only choice.

Though she listened at the connecting door from time to

time, she was unable to hear any sounds at all from Devlyn's side. So at a quarter till seven she made her way to the dining room. Alone.

When Gillian arrived she saw that almost everyone was already seated.

Vincent Wolff stood politely. "Welcome, Ms. Carlyle. I think you know most of us. But we have new additions, I'm proud to report. Gracie, there in the pink, is Gareth's wife, and this sweet young thing to my left is Victor's granddaughter, Cammie, and her mother, Olivia, Kieran's wife."

Fortunately for Gillian, Jacob and his bride were still traveling, and Devlyn and Annalise's brother, Larkin, was not present, either. She didn't think she could have borne the scrutiny of the whole lot of them.

It was bad enough as it was. The feeling of being an outsider was keen and unsettling. Devlyn didn't help matters. He acted as if what had happened that morning in the rain was not even on his radar. And wasn't that the way she wanted it?

If Devlyn had been in a flirtatious mood, she might have embarrassed herself by mooning over him. Instead, she concentrated on chatting with the only other two people at the table who might understand how she felt.

Blue-eyed Gracie, the redhead, was sweet, but quiet. Olivia, on the other hand, was gorgeous, with long brunette hair, a curvaceous figure and flashing dark eyes that sparkled when she laughed.

Gillian exchanged small talk with them and did her best to ignore Devlyn.

Annalise stirred the pot. "So, Gillian, how did my brother come to hire you? I wasn't aware that he had even begun interviews."

All eyes turned to Gillian. Her hands, hidden beneath the table, clenched in her lap. Keeping her words even and matter-of-fact, she answered the pointedly barbed question. "I had a car accident near the bottom of the mountain recently. Devlyn was kind enough to help me when I was stranded. During our conversation I told him that I had lost my teaching job because of budget cutbacks. He realized that I could help out with the new school."

Annalise studied her for long, painful seconds. "How fortunate for you," she drawled, the expression on her face impossible to read.

Devlyn frowned, looking at his sister with irritation. "Knock it off, Annalise. Gillian is a highly qualified teacher and a resident of Burton. She's perfect for the job."

The rest of the table had fallen silent, sensing drama in the making. The two siblings scowled at each other. Annalise seemed unaffected by her brother's ill humor. She turned and smiled at Gillian, a seemingly warm, genuine smile. "Forgive my bad manners. Devlyn and I are in the habit of needling each other. But I usually don't allow collateral damage. I'm glad you'll be working with us."

Gillian was ready to crawl under the table when salvation arrived in the form of Devlyn's taciturn cousin Gareth. The other man stood, putting a hand on his wife's shoulder. "At the risk of sounding unconcerned about the new school, I'd like to get personal for a moment."

He glanced down at his pink-cheeked wife. "We had hoped to say this with everyone present, but that's starting to look like Christmas at the soonest, and some things can't wait." He paused and swallowed, his face radiating quiet joy. "Gracie's pregnant."

Pandemonium erupted. Cammie jumped out of her seat. Victor and Vincent both tried to pretend they weren't wiping away tears. Olivia beamed and Kieran smiled broadly.

No one seemed to notice Devlyn. No one but Gillian. His face froze, every nuance of expression wiped away. For a split second, anguish filled his eyes, a hurt so deep and bitter that

Gillian almost gasped aloud. She started to stand, driven to touch him, to offer comfort.

But in an instant, the grief vanished. In its place was the man with the lazy smile, the affable, bright-eyed life of the party. Devlyn got to his feet, his hands white-knuckled on the back of his chair. "To Gracie," he said, lifting his wineglass. "To Gareth, who won't know what hit him. And to the newest baby Wolff."

Victor glanced at his brother, his beaming grin smug. "That will be two for me. You'd better find someone for those kids of yours, Vincent. You aren't getting any younger."

Vincent took the teasing in good stride, but to Gillian's assessing gaze, his soul was troubled.

Devlyn patted his father's back. "Dad knows the business is my baby. I guess you'd better count on Annalise for grandchildren. She has men hanging all over her. Surely one of them can be hog-tied before they discover what a pain in the butt she is."

Suddenly insults and good-natured teasing flew back and forth across the table in rapid-fire succession. Gillian sat back and watched the interplay, wistfully wishing she had at least one sibling with whom to trade such wicked repartee.

The Wolffs were a warm, tightly knit family.

She caught Devlyn's eye and pointed to her watch. He gathered the crowd's attention for a second time. "I promised Gillian that I would have her home early. Save some dessert for me. I'll expect my piece of pie when I get back."

Beneath a barrage of hoots and catcalls, Devlyn and Gillian said their goodbyes and finally made it out of the room. "I need to get my suitcase and purse," she said.

He barely looked at her. "I'll bring the car around," he said. "Meet me out front in ten minutes."

Despite the distance to her room, she was able to make it there and back quickly. Devlyn tossed her bag in the backseat and slid behind the wheel. Gillian joined him, wincing when he swung out of the portico, causing the tires to slip and spin on the damp pavement.

The rain had moved out. The night was dark, with low clouds obscuring both stars and moon.

Silence lay thick and suffocating inside the small vehicle. Gillian stared out the window, wishing she could disappear. "I'm sorry if I offended you about not wanting to stay for dinner," she said. "But I think my point was well taken. Gareth and Gracie didn't need a stranger present for their big news."

"Clearly, they would be happy for the whole world to know. Forget it."

The darkness made it easier for her to speak her mind. "You're not happy for them."

A heartbeat of hushed shock. "Of course I am."

"I saw your face. Everyone else was looking at Gracie and Gareth. But I was watching you."

"You're imagining things."

In the dark, in the quiet, she was brave. Placing one hand on his hard, muscular thigh, she sighed. "I don't expect anything from you, Devlyn, other than the here and now. But I deserve your honesty. Is that too much to ask before I sneak off to Atlanta with you?"

His hesitation was eons longer this time. "Is that an ultimatum?"

She rubbed his leg. "Of course not. But I can see how much tonight hurt you. And I want to know why."

One mile passed. Two. She sat back in her seat, no longer touching him. If he chose to retreat behind a wall of stony silence, there was nothing she could do about it.

Up ahead, her mother's small house came into view. It was tucked away in a small copse of maples that Gillian's father had planted when Gillian was small. The porch light was on, but the windows were dark. The car rolled to a stop. Devlyn cut the engine.

Gillian fumbled in her purse and found her keys. "I'm sure my mother is asleep. She was up early this morning."

"That's why you didn't want to stay, isn't it? You didn't honestly think anyone would comment on our relationship. You were embarrassed that your mother was cleaning the house while you were a guest."

Gillian knew enough psychology to recognize what was going on. She'd had to take classes as part of her teacher training. Devlyn was trying to shift the onus on to her.

"Yes," she said baldly. "I was embarrassed. It's weird."

"Only in your head. A job is a job. Your mother is a valuable member of the Wolff staff…just as you are now."

She couldn't tell if he was trying to reassure her or put her in her place. "We seem to be blurring the lines," she said. "Maybe if you decide what you want from me, it would be easier."

"Can't I have both? The teacher *and* the woman?"

"God, you're stubborn. I suppose always getting what you want will do that to a man."

He leaned across the console and slid a hand beneath her hair. "I want *you,*" he said, the words gruff. "But since I'm a little too old to be screwing in the backseat of a car in my date's driveway, I suppose I'm doomed to disappointment." He pulled her close and kissed her gently. "Don't analyze this, Gillian. Just live in the moment."

It wasn't her style. It wasn't her preference. But when he touched her breast and lightly rubbed her aching nipple, she allowed herself to be persuaded. "I'll try." She tangled her tongue with his, experiencing the slow, sweet slide into arousal.

Devlyn broke away at long last, breathing hard. "Damned carnival," he muttered.

She smiled in the darkness. "I'll meet you there. My mother will want to come, I'm sure."

"And then Saturday morning, first thing, we're out of here. We'll take the jet." His hoarse words were a vow. "I'll have you in my bed before lunch."

She stiffened instinctively, and he realized what he had said.

Devlyn groaned. "Oh, hell. You won't get on the jet, will you? We'll have to drive. A whole damn day. Maybe we'll go to D.C. instead. It's closer."

She ran her fingers through his hair, dragging his mouth back to hers. "Think of it as foreplay," she whispered. "I'm sure we could get creative if we tried."

Seventeen

Devlyn's mind raced ahead, already imagining Gillian's nimble fingers pleasuring him as they traversed the interstate. Good God.

He pushed her away, breathing heavily. A few more seconds of that and he'd be tumbling her into the backseat. "Go inside," he begged. "Please."

Her soft laugh had the same effect as an electric shock. All the hair on his body stood up, and his heart stopped… beat sluggishly…and finally started again.

She opened her door and squeezed his hand. "I'll bring plenty of cash for the dunking booth," she said. "I like the thought of having you at my mercy."

He shoved her out of the car. It was either that or let her drive him insane with lust. "Good night," he called out through his open window.

As he drove away, he watched her in the rearview mirror, standing guard, tracking his progress as he rolled out of sight.

He took his time getting home. The open road called, offering the oblivion of unknown destinations and endless flight. The prospect of meandering for an hour held a distinct attraction. But his family would be expecting him, and after all they had collectively suffered, he would never deliberately cause them to worry.

The staff was gone for the night when he returned…at least the ones who didn't live on-site. He parked himself in the enormous garage and went outside to look up. Clouds still cloaked the mountaintop. Dampness seeped into his bones.

"I thought you weren't coming back."

His sister's voice startled him. He spun around and spotted a pale figure in the mist. "Still a night owl, I see."

"You expected me to change?"

Now that his eyes had adjusted to the dark, he could make out Annalise perched on a wall, her legs swinging. He shrugged. "None of us ever do, I suppose."

She hopped down. "You want to walk?"

He nodded. Once upon a time this had been their ritual, along with their brother, Larkin. The three of them would slip out late at night and prowl the mountain like a band of wild coyotes.

Annalise put her arm around his waist, rubbing her cheek on his shoulder. "I think *you* may have changed, Devvie. I've never seen you with a woman like Gillian. She's not exactly a looker."

"She's beautiful," he said, disturbed that Annalise couldn't see it. "Like a lush, quiet meadow beneath a hot summer sun."

"My big brother waxing poetic. Will wonders never cease."

He wrapped an arm around her narrow shoulders, tucking her close to his side. "I still maintain that you're a brat."

"Is this serious?"

He swallowed. "No. You know I don't do serious."

"There's always a first time."

"Not for me."

"Have you talked to her?"

"No. It's not important. She and I are enjoying a mutual attraction."

"And when she falls in love with you or vice versa?"

"I won't. And I haven't spun her any promises."

"You're my brother and I love you, but sometimes you're an idiot."

He sighed and turned their steps in the direction of the house. "Takes one to know one."

The following day crawled by. Knowing Gillian, she was up to her ears in the paperwork they had gone over, crossing *t*s and dotting *i*s and making sure not a single detail fell through the cracks. Devlyn wanted badly to call her. The impulse was so strong, he forced himself to ignore it. Her probing the night before, along with the lecture from Annalise, had left him unsettled.

Nothing had changed. *He* hadn't changed. Annalise's worries were unfounded. He had everything under control.

But when he thought about the possibility of opening his heart to Gillian, a tiny glimmer of hope flickered to life inside his chest.

Midmorning he and Annalise drove down to the school site to meet the company that was supplying the inflatable play equipment and the tents for the carnival games. In an hour, volunteers began to arrive, armed with enthusiasm and strong backs.

Annalise was in her element, cheerfully barking out orders and organizing her minions. The day was hot already. Though in Burton they occasionally had snow as early as Halloween, it also wasn't unusual to get a wave of autumn heat that brought out one last hurrah for summer.

Fortunately, this was one of those days.

During a lull in the action when Devlyn's skills and muscle weren't needed, he made his way to the back of the property, disappearing into the woods where he and Gillian had spent time alone yesterday morning.

Simply standing there, near the stump, caused his heart to slug in his chest and his erection to grow rigid with longing. He was a highly sexed man, and he understood the mechanics of male arousal. What he couldn't fathom was the way his chaotic emotions seemed to be taking precedence over his physical need at the moment.

It would be hours before he could take her again. And yet, he was excited at the thought of simply being with her. Eating greasy funnel cakes, winning a gaudy stuffed animal for her at the dart table, holding her hand.

Incredulous at his sappy anticipation, he stared deep into his heart and wondered if Annalise was right. *Was* he changing? Could he?

Shaking off the impossible notion, he strode back to the melee, his chest tight with confusion. All he wanted from Gillian was sex. And that was nothing new for him, not at all.

By four o'clock, it was time for him and his wilting sister to head up the mountain for a shower and a change of clothes. Despite her exhaustion, Annalise chattered the entire way home. She thrived on a challenge, and the day's activities had energized her mentally.

There was an awkward moment when Devlyn insisted on driving his own car down the mountain to the carnival. The rest of the family loaded up without comment, but Annalise gave him a pointed look that said she knew what he was up to.

When they all arrived at the site of the future school, a small crowd began to converge on the once-barren field. First a dozen, then two, then more and more until the place was packed with families out for an evening's entertainment.

It took him thirty minutes to find Gillian. At last he located her in the kissing booth. A husky farmer in overalls handed over a five-dollar bill and planted an enthusiastic smack on Gillian's laughing lips. The line was too long for Devlyn's liking.

He strode to the front without apology, smacked down a twenty, and putting both hands beneath Gillian's hair, kissed her long and slow until the crowd of cheering males demanded their turn.

Ignoring the impatient row of testosterone behind him, he whispered in her ear, "Come find me when you're done."

Her hair was tied up in a ponytail in deference to the heat. It made her look about sixteen. "Sure," she said, her voice breathless. "It won't be long."

He walked away, his barely leashed hunger unable to bear the sight, even in fun, of other men touching her. It was impossible for a Wolff, any one of them, to wander unnoticed. People stopped him time and again to say hello, to offer thanks for the new school to come.

Devlyn felt as if he were watching himself from a distance. He smiled and shook hands and chatted with strangers, all the while impatiently counting the seconds until Gillian arrived at his side.

Little Cammie distracted him for fifteen minutes by enlisting him to challenge her beloved daddy to a game of water pistols. It was the kind of game where each contestant pummeled a small opening and tried to pop a balloon. Kieran had already trounced Gareth and was riding high on his victory.

Devlyn stepped up beside his cousin. "I hate to disappoint your cute-as-a-button daughter, but you're going down."

Kieran flexed both hands and grasped the trigger of his neon-orange plastic revolver. "Bring it on."

The air horn sounded, and both men fired. Devlyn was cool and focused. In his peripheral vision, he could see Kieran grinning as he shot a stream of water in a calculated arc.

Six other men flanked them, but Devlyn knew his cousin was his only competition.

All across the arcade, colorful balloons rose and fattened. It was close, so close. Suddenly, Devlyn felt a small, cool hand touch his left arm. "You're doing great," Gillian cried. "Don't let him win."

Devlyn's trigger finger relaxed for half a second, his attention riveted on her laughing face. Though he immediately returned to the challenge, it was too late. Kieran's balloon popped with a loud report, and Devlyn was forced to eat crow.

He holstered the gun and slung an arm around her shoulders. "Did he bribe you to distract me?" he asked, inhaling her scent, feeling a zing of joy bounce through his chest.

Gillian's gaze met Kieran's. They both grinned.

"I'll never tell," she said, laughing in delight.

Moments later, Devlyn glanced at his watch and realized that his shift at the dunking booth was about to start. Dragging Gillian in his wake, he worked his way to the far side of the field where a metal tank stood, painted in red, white and blue stripes.

He handed her his watch and billfold and started stripping off his clothes. Her eyes widened in shock until she saw that he wore black swim trunks beneath his pants. "Get your money ready," he said.

The line for the dunking booth wound in an arc and doubled back on itself. The teenage boy who preceded Devlyn in the hot seat was a popular quarterback at the consolidated high school. His teammates were ruthless, dunking their friend time and again. The skinny kid was visibly grateful when Devlyn climbed up to relieve him.

Gillian pulled a small, folded stack of ones from her jeans pocket and waited her turn. Devlyn charmed the crowd, entertaining his would-be attackers with hilarious wisecracks.

His broad chest gleamed in the sun, his shoulders wide and sculpted with muscle. When he smiled, Gillian felt the day grow brighter.

Devlyn had been dunked only twice by the time Gillian made it to the front of the line. She took the softball handed to her by the volunteer and eyed her target. The metal circle was about twelve inches in diameter and about fifteen feet away.

Her lover watched, momentarily silent, as she tossed the ball in her hand. Up and down, up and down. Devlyn was shivering, the brisk breeze chilling his skin despite the warm afternoon. His hair was wet. He shoved it back from his forehead with a quick hand, betraying for a split second his impatience.

She smiled. "Here we go."

At a dollar a try, she had enough for twenty shots. But she was out of practice and had trouble finding her rhythm. The first seven dollars she handed over were wasted.

Devlyn sat, arms folded across his chest…cocky, laughing. "Nice try, little girl. Why don't you admit defeat? You'll never do it."

Gillian's temper flickered. Devlyn Wolff might best her in any number of ways, but not this. Not today.

She wound up a pitch and let fly, this one hitting the tank with a thud that made the steel vibrate with a dull *thunk*.

Devlyn hooted. The crowd shouted encouragement.

Gillian took a deep breath, grabbed another ball and steadied herself. This time she hit the target, but it was a glancing blow, not hard enough to engage the mechanism.

Five minutes later she was down to her last dollar, and Devlyn Wolff had become an infuriating, testosterone-driven heckler. Sweat beaded Gillian's forehead. Her hand was slippery. Drying her palms on her jeans, she reached for her final shot.

The ball felt heavy. Her arm ached. Gritting her teeth, she

refused to look at Devlyn this time. Focusing her attention on that small metal target, she reared back, took a deep breath and heaved the softball with all her might.

It hit the circle dead-on and Devlyn yelled in shock as he plunged into the icy water. The crowd went wild. Immediately, he was on his feet, waist-deep in the tank, his hot gaze trapping Gillian's across the heads of children and adults who thronged to hug her and congratulate her.

She smiled at him tauntingly, exulted at her successful attempt to bring him down. But in the pit of her stomach, tiny butterflies were born at the knowledge that retribution would come.

To say the day was a success was an understatement. The crowds stayed late. The weather was perfect. The money rolled in.

But by ten-thirty that night, even the diehards were beginning to call it an evening. Devlyn had kept Gillian by his side for hours, feeding her cotton candy, teasing her about her penchant for Skee-Ball, and being introduced to her neighbors, many of whom had grown up in the valley and stayed as adults.

He was more than ready to tuck her into the car and find some privacy when a red-faced, heavyset woman dashed across the grass intent on intercepting them. "Mr. Wolff, Mr. Wolff," she said. "This is my four-year-old grandson. If construction stays on schedule, he'll be in the first class to go all the way through the new school." She shoved the sleepy-eyed kid into Devlyn's arms. "I want to get a picture of the two of you."

Gillian stepped out of the way, charmed to see the über-masculine Devlyn holding a chubby little boy.

The woman pulled out her camera and held it up. "Smile for Granny."

The little boy managed a grin, but Gillian's amusement faded when she saw Devlyn's face. Instead of staring at the camera, he was looking down at the child in his arms. The expression on his face was terrible to witness.

She blinked, and the moment was gone, almost as if she had conjured it up in her imagination.

Devlyn set the boy on his feet and smiled at the grandma. "Thanks for coming today."

As the woman and her little one wandered off, Gillian linked her arm through Devlyn's, disturbed, but unable to put her finger on any exact cause.

He nuzzled her neck. "Only a few more hours," he said, "and I'll have you all to myself."

"I have good news."

"I'm all ears."

"I went to the walk-in clinic today and got a prescription for motion sickness. The doctor swears by it. So if you're still willing, I'd like to take the jet."

Eighteen

Devlyn sighed. "Thank goodness. All those hours locked up in a car with you would have tested my control."

She linked her fingers with his. "Am I that irresistible?"

"You have no idea." He glanced around, assessing the level of privacy. He and Gillian were a good hundred yards from the nearest carnival enthusiast, but that was still too crowded for what he had in mind. "Follow me," he said, tugging on her hand.

She cooperated without protest. Which boded well for the weekend's plans. A compliant woman made a man imagine all sorts of scenarios. He stopped in front of the first-aid tent and looked casually over his shoulder. No one was paying any attention. Holding back the flap, he ushered Gillian inside and ducked beneath the canvas. "Alone at last."

All the medical supplies had already been cleared out, but a cot remained. In the dark, he could hear Gillian breathe. "We are *not* going to do this," she said firmly.

"Do what?"

"You know what I mean."

He tracked her by feel, running his hands over her shoulders and pulling her close. "I can't wait till Atlanta. I tried. But I can't."

"We're going there in the morning."

"Seems like forever." He kissed her forehead. But his hands were busy, too. Her breasts fit his palms perfectly. She was wearing a simple, thin T-shirt, and he could feel the firm thrust of her nipples against his fingertips.

"Devlyn…" Her voice came as a soft sigh in the darkness. Wrapping her arms around his neck, she found his mouth with hers, both of them hungry…impatient.

He ripped her T-shirt up and off, shoving the bra aside to taste sweet curves, the soft flesh crowned with rigid, berrylike nubs. Gillian trembled in his arms. She was slender, delicate, so sweet.

"Wait." He dragged himself away from her and peered outside the tent. The field was empty and quiet now save for the various booths and tents that would be dismantled in the morning. All the cars were gone. Thank God.

Gillian had definitely lost her shyness with him. Her slim, strong fingers wrapped around his wrist and pulled. "Hurry," she said.

He knelt in front of her and dragged her jeans and panties down her legs. Gillian kicked them aside and pressed herself, naked as the day she was born, to his chest. *Sweet Lord.*

He scooped her into his arms and carried her four steps to the cot. Depositing her gently, he disposed of his own clothes and came down on top of her, using his hands to spread her thighs. The makeshift bed was narrow. Devlyn was big and desperate.

Canvas and metal creaked and popped as he fit himself to Gillian's warm, welcoming center. When the head of his shaft slid inside, his brain shut down. He had a faint sensation that something was not right, but he ignored it like brushing away a pesky fly. The only thing left was sensation. Wet silk wrapped around an erection that was as hard as ones he'd sported as a callow teen.

He wanted to say things to her…needed her to know what this meant to him. But his body betrayed him. Need was a razor-sharp enemy, tying him in knots, urging him to take… take…take. Thrusting firmly, he buried himself all the way to her core.

Gillian's legs wrapped around his waist.

"Am I crushing you?" He could barely push the words from his dry throat.

"No," she whispered. "You're perfect."

Her response made him flinch inwardly, but there was no time for self-analysis. Beneath him, she was soft and welcoming…intensely feminine. He moved in her, feeling something beyond the connection of body to body. Without words, she offered healing where he had asked for none.

He loved her slowly, drawing every moment into a million shattered sparkles of bliss. Something shifted inside him, a momentous fault line grinding open to reveal weakness he had never allowed anyone to see.

Even now, he couldn't share it. Not with her. Not with pure, decent Gillian. But he acknowledged its existence. Faced it down. Stood strong.

He would not be broken. Not with so much at stake.

Gillian's inner muscles clenched his shaft as she cried out. The extra stimulation was more than he could bear. He shouted as he climaxed, shuddering, helpless, spent and dazed in her arms.

Gillian stirred, wondering if she had dozed off. "Devlyn. I have to go home."

His rough tongue found her nipple and sent ripples of re-membered pleasure skating through her veins.

She shoved at his chest. "Seriously. Let me up."

He mumbled a protest but finally levered himself to his feet. Darkness was Gillian's salvation, enabling her to dress without his slumberous eyes luring her into another round of insanity.

Muttering an imprecation when his head bumped a tent pole, Devlyn dressed, as well. She could barely see him. "What time is it?" she asked.

He hit a button and illuminated the dial of his watch. "After midnight."

"Good grief."

"Don't worry," he said, a smile in his voice. "I'll let you sleep in. Be ready at ten. We'll be in Atlanta for a late lunch."

Her heart skipped a beat. Was she deliberately going to accompany this virile, amazing man to his luxurious home in Georgia for the sole purpose of having sex over and over again?

God help her, she was. Because she was infatuated with him. It was pointless to deny it or to pretend that he wasn't going to break her heart. The knowledge hurt. Badly. And her reckless avoidance of dealing with reality was blatantly uncharacteristic.

But she would have Devlyn all to herself. And for the moment, that was enough.

He held her hand as they walked back across the grass to the car. With the sun long gone, the air was chilled, the night shadowy and still. Though Devlyn was not a man for pretty speeches, she believed he cared about her.

But was that a lie she had invented to pave the way for her upcoming foolishness, or was it true? Did he see her as anything other than a convenient bed partner?

Troubled and unsettled, she allowed him to tuck her into the car. Her mother's house was only a few miles away. They completed the trip in silence, each lost in thought.

Though she protested, he insisted on walking her to the door. As before, the house was dark, the porch light left on for late arrivals.

They faced each other on the top step. She cleared her throat. "I'll be ready in the morning."

His sexy smile was nowhere to be seen. The expression on his face could best be described as somber. "Tell me you understand this is not a permanent liaison."

Agony ripped through her chest, stealing her soul, her breath. "Has Annalise been warning you about me? Don't worry, Devlyn. I'm under no illusions."

His thumbs brushed her cheeks with butterfly caresses. "If it were anybody, it would be you." They were so close she could inhale the scent of lovemaking on his skin.

"Don't," she said curtly, rigid in his embrace…unable to bear tenderness in the midst of cold, hard reality. "I don't need anything from you but your body. I'm a temporarily employed elementary schoolteacher with my life mapped out in front of me. For once, I'm planning to stray from the straight and narrow. Your conscience can remain clear."

The muscles in his throat moved. "I may be condemned to hell for this."

"For what?"

"Taking what you're offering and giving nothing in return."

"Sex for barter is prostitution. And I won't let that happen. Mutual pleasure, Devlyn. That's what this is. Now go home and I'll see you in a few hours."

A sudden noise behind her startled her badly. She whirled around in time to see a small boy scuttle from behind the porch swing. His cheekbone was bloody and bruised, his eyes huge with apprehension. "Ms. Gillian. I wanted to go to the carnival, but I couldn't. Did you bring any cotton candy home with you?"

Gillian glanced at Devlyn, whispering sotto voce. "It's Jamie. My mother takes him to Sunday school on the weekends. He lives on a farm down the road." A wretched, run-down place with wrecked cars in the yard and a roof missing shingles.

The boy was somewhere between four and five years of age. But he was small and thin and had the look of malnutrition.

She crouched in front of him. "I'm sorry, Jamie. There wasn't any cotton candy left over. Why couldn't you come tonight?"

He rubbed his unhurt eye. "My daddy needed me to work."

"To work?"

"I have to help feed the animals."

Something didn't ring true. "What happened to your face? Did you fall down?"

Big eyes looked up at her, their gaze oddly adult. "Yeah. That was it."

He was lying. She knew it as well as she knew her name. "Who hurt you, Jamie?" she asked softly, putting a hand on his arm.

He flinched and backed away, breaking the contact. "No one."

Gillian expected Devlyn to step in any moment and help her, but he stood silent and unmoving. Trying to keep her voice reassuring, she asked again, "Who hit your face, Jamie? You can trust me. I won't let them do it again."

Hope. Painful, flickering hope spread over his face. Those wary, cagey eyes darted to Devlyn and back to Gillian. "He said I deserved it."

Oh, God. "Who, Jamie? Your dad?"

Huge, silent tears welled in his eyes and made tracks down his dirty cheeks. He nodded, unable to say the words.

"Where is he now?"

"Asleep. I can count," he said with tragic pride. "When I see five bottles I know he won't wake up. That's why I ran away."

Gillian stood and turned to Devlyn. "Help me get him into the house," she said, speaking quietly so the boy couldn't hear. "He may need stitches."

Devlyn didn't move. "No." In the pale, yellowish light from the single bulb by the door, his features were a mask, totally devoid of emotion. Even his eyes were dull and lifeless. "Call the police. They have procedures to deal with these situations. Social services."

Everything inside her congealed with horrified disbelief. He wasn't going to lift a finger for either her or for the boy. "I know you don't like children," she whispered furiously, "but damn it, Devlyn, this is low. Are you really such a cold-hearted bastard?"

Her heart broke as her dreams shattered. She beseeched him with her eyes and her sheer will. "Tell me you'll stay and help me deal with whatever has to happen."

He shrugged. "I have things to do. It's late. Call 911 and they'll pick him up." Turning his back on her, he walked down the steps calmly.

Everything inside her throbbed with a pain so intense, she felt faint. "Devlyn," she shouted at him, torn by anger and desperation and incredulity.

He stopped, hesitated, turned. "What?" Without the light to illuminate his face, he was nothing more than a shape in the dark.

"If you walk away right now, don't bother to come for me in the morning."

She didn't mean to say it. She wanted to snatch back the words as soon as they left her mouth. It was a test. An ultimatum. Perhaps he couldn't, wouldn't, give her the possibility of something real. But surely she hadn't misjudged him this badly. Surely he was an honorable, decent man.

Across the distance of several feet that might as well have been the chasm of the Grand Canyon, they stared at each other. His hands were in his pockets. One large shoulder lifted and fell in a shrug that indicated nothing more than a fillip of regret. "It's probably for the best, Gillian. Good night."

Nineteen

The next hours passed in a blur of exhaustion. Gillian coaxed Jamie into the house, woke her mother, and between the two of them, they fed him and cleaned his cheek and the rest of his small body. With the blood wiped away, the cut was less worrisome. They covered it with antiseptic cream and a small Band-Aid.

The sheriff who arrived less than thirty minutes later was a gentle, soft-spoken man who got down on his knees and eyed Jamie face-to-face. "You see this badge, son?"

Jamie nodded, his little eyes heavy with sleep.

The man picked him up gently. "This badge means I'm going to keep you safe, no matter what."

"Am I gonna stay with Ms. Gillian?"

"No. But somewhere just as good. I know a family that loves little boys like you. They'll feed you and laugh with you and play games and take care of you while the grown-ups make some decisions."

Jamie yawned, his head coming to rest on a shoulder covered in a uniform shirt. "Okay. But do you think *they* might have some cotton candy?"

At 2:00 a.m. Doreen Carlyle looked at her daughter with concern. "Go to bed, honey. Don't worry about Jamie. You did the right thing. He'll be fine."

Gillian bowed her head. Locked up inside her was a torrent of hurt and desolation waiting to pour out. She loved her mother. And the two of them were very close.

But some things were too painful for words. "I know, Mama. But it's still hard." She stood up, feeling shattered... lost. "Good night. I'm sorry I had to wake you."

Doreen followed her down the hall, pausing in her bedroom doorway. "I can go in late. They'll understand." She stopped suddenly, her expression arrested. "How did you get home tonight? Didn't Devlyn bring you? Did he see Jamie?"

Gillian lied, unable to admit to her own mother that the man she had fallen in love with was a spineless, uncaring jerk. "Devlyn had already driven away. He didn't know Jamie was there."

Turning away, she entered her bedroom, shut the door, climbed into bed and cried herself to sleep.

As the hours passed, she mourned. How could she have been so wrong about Devlyn? Evidently the old maxim was true. Love made you blind.

She told herself she hadn't really fallen in love with him. How could she? How was it possible to have any tender feelings at all for a man who was soulless...lacking in compassion, utterly hard and self-centered?

The sex they had shared was nothing but carnal lust. Remembering the feel of his sure hands on her body was a mistake. Because even knowing what she knew now, she still craved his touch.

* * *

Gradually, sanity returned, overriding the huge blanket of self-pity under which she wallowed. Perhaps she was painfully self-deceptive…engulfed in circuitous rationalizations, but she began to be convinced that something was terribly wrong with her assessment of what had happened the night of the carnival.

She *knew* Devlyn, she really did. First as a child and a young adult from a distance, and now as a grown man with strengths and failings just like every other human being. He had helped her when she needed it…he had helped other women in his past, even those who didn't deserve his generosity.

Devlyn was kind and decent and caring. He was not a man who turned his back on those who suffered. So why Jamie? It didn't make sense. Because of that conundrum, on Tuesday morning, she dragged herself out of the doldrums, dressed in a simple long-sleeve jersey wrap dress in forest green and drove up to the castle.

Annalise opened the front door, clearly prepared to leave the premises. Her suitcases were stacked in a pile, ready to be loaded into a car. "What are you doing here?" she asked, her expression less than welcoming.

"I need to see Devlyn. I've finished all the paperwork he gave me, but it has to be signed." She clutched the pile of folders to her chest. "Will you please tell me how to find him?"

Annalise frowned. "I thought you went with him to Atlanta."

"No."

The two women stared at each other. Annalise frowned. "He told me at the carnival Friday night that he was taking you home with him for a romantic getaway. I said it was a bad idea."

"Well, goody for you. Obviously he listened." Gillian felt

the hot sting of tears and the urge to run. But something held her feet in place. Some inexplicable certainty that Devlyn was in crisis. Friday night, standing on her front porch, he had seemed like a walking dead man. And she didn't know why. "Did you actually see him Saturday morning before he left?"

"He was gone before any of us woke up. What happened? What did you do to him?" Now Annalise was alarmed, which made no sense, because clearly a man like Devlyn was not a fragile flower in need of protection, especially from his sister.

"Nothing."

"That's a lie. He wouldn't have left without saying goodbye to all of us unless he was deep into *I've-got-a-new-woman-to-sleep-with* mode."

"So he does this often?"

"What do you think? He's one of the richest men in the world. He's handsome and charming and sexy as hell. I think you know the answer to that."

The confirmation hurt. "Things are different now," Gillian said, trying to make herself believe it. "Something happened. We had a fight. And I don't have time to explain, but I think Devlyn needs me. Please, Annalise." The tears spilled over. "I care about him. And that may not make any difference to you or to him, but at least let me make sure he's okay. He was upset when he left. Not angry, or pissed off…more like frozen, wounded. You know he shuts people out."

Annalise stared at her. "God, I hope you're telling me the truth. 'Cause if not, he'll never forgive me for what I'm about to do."

Gillian placed the folders on a side table and ran her hands up and down her arms, trying to still the shivers of dread. "What do you mean?"

"I'm going to take you to him. On the jet, since Devlyn drove. And you'd better fix whatever's wrong, or I'll make your life hell."

Oddly, Annalise's scowling threat made Gillian want to smile. Devlyn's sister was a tigress, a fierce protector of those she loved. "If he doesn't want me there, I'll go home," Gillian said calmly, lying through her teeth. The only way she would leave Atlanta was if Devlyn made her believe, beyond the shadow of a doubt, that he was perfectly okay and that he had no feelings for her at all.

His cold, irrational reaction to Jamie had to be a symptom of something deeper, darker. And whatever that *something* was, it had caused him to give up the possibility of having a wife and a family. Gillian was willing to stake her pride and her future on it.

It was possible he would throw her out. Or worse, look at her with pity. It *could* play out that way. In which case, Gillian was setting herself up for more heartache. But some things were worth fighting for, and Devlyn Wolff was at the top of Gillian's list, even if he could never give her the family she wanted.

Annalise exhibited single-minded determination once she was convinced about a course of action. After a quick stop at the foot of the mountain for Gillian to throw a few things in a suitcase, they were off. The Wolff family jet sat on a narrow runway at a tiny regional airport. In Annalise's wake, Gillian boarded, feeling as if she was going to her doom… in more ways than one.

The luxury and comfort of the flight couldn't outweigh her distress, even with medication. Nerves and anxiety reduced her to a panicked mess. She barely held herself together. At last, she slept.

Annalise woke her up when they landed in Atlanta. "We're here. The limo is waiting. After I drop you off, I'm headed back to Charlottesville."

Gillian sat up and fumbled in her purse for a comb. "How

do I get in?" They were both making the silent assumption that her assault on Devlyn had to be surreptitious.

As they made the move from the jet to the car, Annalise handed her two items. "The key card is for the penthouse elevator. The actual key opens Devlyn's door. I stay here with him occasionally. I'll introduce you to the doorman when we get there so he won't give you any trouble."

Gillian sat back, mind numb, and surveyed the streets of Atlanta as the chauffeur whisked his passengers along, their tired bodies cradled in soft leather seats. She had never been to the sprawling city, and she fell in love with its tree-lined charm and spectacular skyline. Annalise was silent as well, brooding, her eyes fixed on the scenery.

Devlyn's home sat atop a sleek, super-sophisticated building in the heart of Buckhead, one of Atlanta's premier districts. High-end stores and specialty shops jostled cheek by jowl with unique restaurants and art galleries. Any other time, Gillian would have felt the urge to explore. Today all she could think about was whether she had made a terrible mistake.

Annalise was true to her word. After a brief conversation with a uniformed attendant, she eyed Gillian steadily. "I love my brother," she said. Her chin wobbled. "Don't give up on him."

For a moment, it seemed as if the two women might hug. But Gillian was too frazzled and Annalise too prickly. "I'll do my best."

Then Annalise was gone, and it was all up to Gillian. She crossed the swanky atrium and stopped in front of the nearest gold-door elevator. Thankfully, it was empty. She stepped inside, her knees shaky, and inserted the key card. The rapid *whoosh* as the small, mirrored box rose upward was not at all helpful to the state of her stomach.

With a quiet *ding* she reached her destination. In the hushed, empty foyer, Devlyn's was the only door.

She took out the key, and her hand froze, hovering over the doorknob. What if he had a woman inside? What if he was entertaining? Was she about to humiliate herself beyond reason?

Some invisible force urged her forward, despite her misgivings. Sliding the key into the keyhole, she turned the knob. It opened easily. She slipped inside and closed the door behind her.

For a long moment, she simply took stock. Immediately in front of her sat an elegant narrow table against a wall. On it, a pot of mauve orchids bloomed gracefully. Devlyn's keys lay beside the flowers, tossed carelessly on the polished surface. Gillian recognized the keychain. It was sterling silver, fashioned in the head of a wolf…which meant that, theoretically, the Wolff was home. Setting her purse and suitcase beneath the table, she went in search of the man she had come to confront.

The condo had to be at least several thousand square feet in size. As she rounded the wall, she sucked in a breath of appreciation. Opposite her, across a sea of plush, sand-colored carpet, an entire expanse of glass provided a magnificent view out over the heart of the city.

The elegant space, clearly meant for entertaining, was furnished with an array of sofas and armchairs. But the room was empty.

With a wing of the apartment to the left and right, Gillian was stymied. She listened intently, but could hear no sound from any corner. Her first guess turned out to be wrong. She discovered an amazing kitchen and a trio of guest rooms, each with its own bathroom. But no Devlyn.

As she reversed her steps and headed toward what must be his private quarters on the other side, her heart beat faster. The first door she came to in the hallway was open. She glanced inside and saw a neatly made bed. But on the night-stand was a phone that looked like Devlyn's. Over a chair in the corner was the shirt he had worn to the carnival. But still no sign of him.

Feeling worry mount with every step, she walked on, coming to a stop in the doorway of a large man-cave. A Schwarzenegger movie flickered silently on the far wall. The enormous flat-screen TV dominated the room. But it couldn't hold Gillian's attention. Because stretched out on a long leather sofa, dead to the world, lay Devlyn Wolff.

He was sleeping on his back. At first glance, she saw that he hadn't shaved since he left her standing on her mother's porch. His hair was wet, indicating a recent shower. He was naked but for a white towel tied loosely around his narrow hips. His sex made a noticeable mound beneath the cloth.

The sight of him paradoxically soothed and alarmed her. He was a beautiful man. His head, arms and torso were per-fectly proportioned, his big, hair-dusted thighs made to cra-dle a woman's body. She approached him quietly, her shoes making no sound at all on the carpet that matched the floor-ing in the living room. It wouldn't have mattered in any case. Devlyn slept deeply, his heavy slumber aided no doubt by the contents of the many liquor bottles strewn over the surface of the coffee table.

A trio of empty pizza boxes on the floor was the only sign that his uncharacteristic bender had at least included food. Had he simply gone to ground, hiding out from humanity? Did the office in Atlanta think he was on Wolff Mountain? The reverse had certainly been true according to Annalise. Nudging aside the pile of cardboard with her foot, Gillian sat down on the table.

Praying that she was doing the right thing, she put her hand on his knee. "Wake up, Devlyn."

Twenty

Devlyn groaned, wondering why in the hell the pizza boy was bothering him. Devlyn had left a fifty on the table in the entranceway. That was a damned good tip.

"Devlyn. Look at me."

Opening his eyes was a mistake. The light pierced his skull with agonizing precision. Lord in heaven. He squinted, trying to clear his vision. There, not two feet away, sat the woman who was responsible for his current condition. Or maybe she was a dream. He'd had plenty of those in the last few days. A few of them the kind that left him spent and mentally aching for something beyond his grasp.

"Go away," he muttered. "You're not real." He closed his eyes.

Those same cool fingers nudged his kneecap, making the hair on his legs rise with gooseflesh. "I've come a long way to see you, Devlyn. I need you to sit up."

Most of the time her strict schoolmarm voice turned him

on. Today it was just aggravating. "No one invited you. If you're real, get out."

He put his hands on the sides of his head, groaning. Getting drunk was a stupid stunt, one he'd not indulged in since he was a kid in college. And getting drunk over a *woman* was even dumber. Even if the woman did have big brown eyes and a mouth that could tempt a saint.

When he thought he could bear it, he opened his eyes again. Gillian was still there. She stared at him unblinking. "You want to talk about it?"

"There's nothing to say. If you're not going to leave, I'm going to have sex with you."

She blinked once. "Okay."

Her calm acceptance caught him off guard. "I'm serious," he said, not sure he could walk across the room, much less perform sexually.

"I'll do whatever you want, Devlyn," she said quietly. "But I won't leave."

He sat up, fighting nausea. He must have looked like hell, because she took pity on him. "Get dressed," she said. "I'll go make coffee."

"Whatever." He felt no compunction about his boorish behavior. No one asked her to barge in.

She was gone for fifteen minutes. When she came back bearing a tray with a carafe and two mugs, the smell alone almost made him cry uncle. But not quite. He hadn't shown weakness to a woman in years, and he wouldn't start now.

Gillian paused in the doorway, assessing the fact that he was still wearing a towel. "Aren't you cold?"

"No." God, no. Not with Gillian approaching him wearing a dress that made the most of her modest curves. He stood, determined to face her like a man. Beneath the towel, his sex flexed and lengthened.

She noticed. And almost bobbled the glassware as she set

down the tray. When she straightened, he made himself wait five seconds to grab a cup of the steaming, fragrant lifeline. As he sipped it, he stared at her over the rim. "I see you're still here."

"Yes. I was worried about you."

He shrugged, burning his throat with the speed at which he gulped the hot liquid. "As you can see, I'm fine."

"Are you, Devlyn? Are you really? Because from where I'm standing, you don't look fine at all."

He finished the coffee, set the cup on the table and removed the towel with a flick of his wrist. "Sofa or bedroom. You pick." The silent compassion in her gaze raked his soul like a thousand razor blades. He hadn't asked her to care…didn't want her to. "So you're just going to let me screw you?" he said. "After I distinctly heard you say not to ever come back."

"I didn't understand."

"And now you do?"

"Not really…no. But I realize that something in your past has hurt you deeply. And I want you to know that I'm sorry. Sorry for telling you not to come back. Sorry I didn't try to see things from your perspective."

"Jesus, Gillian. What kind of woman lets a man treat her like crap and comes back for more?" He heard the words leave his mouth and was appalled. But she was ripping away at layers of armor he had honed by fire over the years, and her empathy was starkly, agonizingly painful.

"The kind of woman who might be in love with you." A single tear trickled down her pale cheek, increasing his pain. Her gaze was wounded, but steady.

Fury erupted, refusing to acknowledge that his heart was bleeding. "Take off your dress." If he pushed her hard enough, surely she would leave.

She stared at him for long seconds. Then, after stepping out of her low-heeled pumps, she lifted the dress over her head and tossed it on the nearest chair. Without panty hose or a slip, the only things left were her modest bra and underpants.

Her arms hung at her sides. Though he had known her to blush on more than one occasion, at the moment, she appeared completely self-assured. Which pissed him off even more.

He was acting like a jerk. Couldn't she see that?

"You're not done." He infused the words with determination. "I want you naked."

The brief seconds that passed while watching her slide the bra down her arms and unhook it were torture. When she pushed her simple cotton briefs down her legs and stepped out of them, a groan escaped him.

Since his feet appeared to be nailed to the floor, Gillian walked to where he stood. She held out her arms, embraced him and cradled his head on her shoulder. "I could love you, Devlyn, very easily." Soft fingers feathered through his hair.

He felt himself shudder inside, a huge quaking rift that he couldn't acknowledge, dared not examine. Thirty seconds passed. Then thirty more. With her smooth, soft body pressed to his—her tenderness wrapped around him like a cloud—he almost cracked.

But the consequences were too terrible to contemplate. He jerked out of her arms, blind with a befuddled rage. "I don't want you to," he said. A piercing headache squeezed his temples. He bent and swiped his arm across the coffee table, sending heavy glass bottles flying.

Gillian watched him, arms wrapped around her waist, her eyes tragic.

He took her wrist, drawing her forward. "Last chance."

Any second now, she would slap his face…run out of the room.

But she didn't. Instead, she lay down gracefully on the sofa, her hand outstretched. "It's okay, Devlyn. Everything's okay. I'm here."

The pain in his head had escaped and now filled his entire body. Seeing her like this was more than he could bear. With a roar of confusion, he moved on top of her, fit himself to her core and pushed. Gillian gasped softly, but otherwise was silent. Her legs wrapped around his waist, and she held him tightly as he lunged into her once…twice…three times. He moaned a curse, filling her with his seed.

In the aftermath, he felt tears sting his eyes.

His stomach curled in revulsion. What had he done? Raining kisses of apology over her face and throat, he waited for her to reject him, to curse him.

Instead, she kissed him back, wrapping her fists in his hair and pulling him closer to her. Chest to chest. Breath to breath.

Aching remorse and regret flailed him. It wasn't her fault the situation was untenable. Breaking the kiss suddenly, he lifted himself off her and scooped her into his arms. His bedroom, mere steps away, seemed impossibly far. But he made it somehow.

Striding to the huge bed, he flung back the covers with one hand and laid her gently on the black silk sheets. He slid in beside her. "I'm sorry, Gillian. I'm so sorry."

She put a hand on his chin, forcing him to look into her eyes, eyes that were huge and troubled, but not condemnatory. "Make love to me," she pleaded. "Let me have all of you."

What she asked was dangerous and almost impossible. But he wanted to try. The yearning to drown in her forgiveness was unbearable. "Close your eyes," he muttered.

Gillian obeyed, wondering if he was capable of giving her what she needed…what they *both* needed. Total honesty. Complete intimacy. His trust.

She flinched when she felt the slightly rough stroke of his tongue on her nipples. He loved them one at a time, licking and sucking and pulling each one between his teeth and biting gently.

The erotic punishment filled her belly with a million butterflies and made her legs part restlessly, her body aching for that part of him that could offer her release.

Her fingernails scored his back involuntarily as fire shot though her pelvis and made her moan. It was too much and not enough.

"I want *you*," she begged. "Please. I can't wait."

He pushed her higher and higher, past the point of insanity, drawing out each teasing caress until she was desperate for the climax that hovered just out of reach. She fought wildly, trying to force him into her. But he was heavy and heartbreakingly tender.

When she knew that she was absolutely going to explode in frustration, he entered her. A smooth, determined, thorough penetration. Her breath lodged in her throat. Her heart stopped. Every cell in her body trembled on the cusp of a terrible, wonderful, unprecedented orgasm.

"Devlyn…" It was a whisper, a plea, a prayer.

He answered her instantly, gruffly. "Now, baby." Withdrawing completely, he slammed into her with a forceful thrust that smashed through some unseen barrier and sent her careening into bliss.

His big, hard body trembled violently as he shouted her name, pistoning his hips in his own out-of-control, shuddering release.

Gillian tried to pin down a single emotion but could not. Joy. Fear. Worry. Momentary contentment.

What was he thinking? Still on top of her, his sweat-dampened body was a deadweight. The time of reckoning had come.

"Please tell me, Devlyn. Why did you run away from Jamie?"

He didn't challenge her description of his actions. But he rolled to his back and slung an arm over his eyes. "He was me," he muttered.

She frowned, drawing the sheet up to her throat and holding it in a death grip. "I don't know what you mean." But the sick feeling in her stomach told her that she did.

Devlyn's chest heaved. Still he didn't look at her. "When I was Jamie's age, my mother had been slapping me around for a couple of years."

The flat, almost desolate intonation in his voice hurt something in Gillian's chest. Though she couldn't think of a single response to his horrific statement, he kept talking.

"When she drank, she liked to hit. No broken bones, no weapon but the back of her hand. I was the oldest, and I had to protect Larkin and Annalise. In truth, I don't know if she would have gone after them anyway. I seemed to inspire her fury."

He rolled out of bed suddenly and paced. "She would scream at me and back me into a corner. My father never knew, or so he says. He was working long hours away from the house."

"Oh, God, Devlyn." He didn't seem to hear her.

"Sometimes she used lit cigarettes on me. That was the worst." Unconsciously, it seemed, he rubbed a series of tiny, almost unnoticeable scars at his hip. "I never cried out. I didn't want my brother and sister to come running."

Gillian sat up, shaking uncontrollably. The fact that Devlyn was naked made his terrible monotone even worse. She had forced him to tell her this awful secret. She had stripped him bare.

She didn't want to hear any more, but it was too late to staunch the flow of ragged, hoarse words.

His hands fisted at his hips. The cords in his neck stood out in relief. "It all happened before Wolff Mountain. Dad and Uncle Vic were close, even then. Built houses side by side in a ritzy neighborhood in Charlottesville. Sometimes if it got too bad, I would run next door to Aunt Laura. She would tend to me, cry over me. I didn't understand then or later why she didn't try to stop it. But she was young...maybe scared. I don't know."

"And Annalise and Larkin?"

"Sometimes late at night they would climb into my bed and curl up against me. They felt helpless...like I did."

She swallowed. "So that day in the cave when you said you hated her and you were glad she was gone, you meant it."

For the first time, his gaze locked with hers, his eyes burning dark in an ashen face. "I did. And you looked at me like I was a monster. I didn't blame you. What kind of kid wants his mother to die?"

"Devlyn, I—"

He held up a hand, cutting her off. "I know what I am, Gillian. I'm damaged goods. And someone like you deserves a whole man, the kind of man who can make promises to you and keep them."

"Nothing that happened was your fault. Surely you know that."

He shrugged. "I saw a counselor...in college. All the Wolff kids studied under assumed names, because Dad and Uncle Vic were afraid we'd be kidnapped like our mothers had been. Since no one knew who I really was, there was no risk of anyone finding out about the Wolff family's dirty secrets."

"What did the counselor say?"

"That I had turned into a fine young man, and that I needed to put the past behind me."

Gillian said a word that she had never used out loud in her life. "That's criminal. You can't pretend abuse never happened."

"A lot of people do that. They literally block it out. It's a coping mechanism."

"But you couldn't do that."

"Maybe if she hadn't died. Maybe if I hadn't wished her dead a million times."

"Devlyn, you were a baby. And she hurt you. A mother's sacred duty is to protect her children, but she failed you."

"Who knows why she did what she did. But the counselor was right in a way. I *did* have to put it behind me and move on. And I have."

"How? How can you say that, when I see you standing in front of me bleeding and hurt…after all these years?"

His bleak smile chilled her soul. "I'm lucky. My scars are mostly on the inside. And I had a solid family to help me get through the aftermath of the kidnappings. That kid, Jamie? He's got nothing but poverty and a long road to nowhere."

Gillian got out of bed clumsily, the sheet wrapped toga-style around her. Devlyn didn't move as she approached him. Like a stone statue, he was rigid, immovable.

She stood toe-to-toe with him, searching his face. "That's not all, is it? Why can't you let me into your life for more than a casual fling? I think you care about me, somehow… at some level. But why is that so threatening?"

Even the flame of suffering in his eyes flickered out. Now he was nothing but a weary shell of a man. "You're the kind of woman who needs a home and a family. I can only break your heart, because I don't have one. I don't want to have one. After I lost my virginity—after I was so scared that I had gotten a married woman pregnant—it dawned on me that a vindictive husband would have been the least of my worries."

"How?"

"Child abuse is cyclical in nature. I'd cut off my arm before I would allow any child of mine to run that risk. So you're wasting your time, Gillian. Don't love me. Because I can't love you back."

"Can't? Or won't?"

He stared down at her, perhaps unaware of the longing etched on his face. "Doesn't really matter, does it?"

"I think it does. Wake up, Devlyn. Smell the coffee. You just made love to me twice. Without protection."

He went white. And for the first time she understood that the man whose home she'd invaded had been so traumatized by his confrontation with Jamie, that he had literally been defenseless when she forced a showdown.

Oh, Lordy. She straightened her shoulders. "If I am pregnant, I expect you to marry me." She said it calmly, though her emotions were anything but. Did she really have the guts to blackmail a Wolff?

Hell, yes. She was fighting for their future.

The muscles in his throat worked, betraying his agitation. "That monster is still inside me," he croaked. "I wanted my mother to die. Don't you understand that?"

Here it was. The final truth. "I do, Devlyn. I do. But I also believe that you loved her anyway…didn't you?"

Silence fell, an enormous raw void filled only by two sets of thundering hearts.

Wolffs didn't show weakness. And they surely didn't cry. Not as adult men. But when Devlyn broke at last and grabbed her, he held her as if she were the only steady footing in his universe.

Devlyn felt at peace, and marveled at the sensation. The tentative acceptance of healing humbled him. This brave, selfless woman standing clasped in his arms had accomplished the impossible. For one final painful moment he allowed himself to remember his mother's face. Who knew what demons tormented her? Who knew why no one stepped in to protect a little boy?

He would never know. But it was okay.

Feeling like he'd survived a war, he stroked Gillian's silky hair, her soft back, the curve of her ass. "I didn't do it on purpose," he said, his eyes damp.

"Do what?"

Somehow, he'd had the good fortune to dispense with the sheet between them. He'd never felt anything more wonderful than Gillian's naked body against his. "I didn't forget the condoms on purpose, I swear."

She rubbed the small of his back, soothing him, arousing him.

"I believe you."

"Unless my subconscious is a devious son of a bitch."

She chuckled. "Would you mind terribly? If we made a baby today?"

Hearing her say it aloud constricted his throat almost beyond speech. Imagining Gillian, her belly round with his daughter...or son... Dear God. "I wouldn't mind." There was so much more he wanted to say, but the words wouldn't come.

Gillian seemed to understand, her heart more nimble than his, more generous.

Still, he owed her more than cowardice. "I won't let you down, I swear. But you'll call my hand? If you ever see me start to do something to our child..." He stumbled to a halt, the notion unbearable.

She pinched his butt. She actually pinched his butt.

"Don't be ridiculous," she said. "You would never use your strength to harm anyone, especially a child." She took his face in her two hands. "I don't think that, Devlyn. I *know* it."

He saw the absolute confidence in her eyes and nodded, struggling to accept the truth that had eluded him for so long. "I've fallen in love with you, Gillian. In every way there is to love a woman. I didn't know that I could, but you burrowed your way into my life and my heart so quickly I never saw it coming."

Seeing the hesitance on her face was his well-deserved punishment. He had put it there, and it would be up to him to make sure she never doubted him again.

She wrinkled her nose. "You don't have to say that. I know you've been through a lot. But I can wait until you're sure."

He put his hand on her flat abdomen, stepping back to look at her from head to toe. "You're going to be a gorgeous pregnant woman," he said, mentally opening up to the fierce joy that swelled in his chest. "And I can prove that I love you." He picked her up and carried her to the bed, cradling her like infinitely precious treasure.

"How?" Her uncertainty dragged at his heart.

Dropping her unceremoniously and standing back to enjoy the view, he put his hands on his hips. "You're the only woman I've ever had sex with in this condo. And I've lived here a long, long time."

Her eyes narrowed. "You expect me to believe that?"

He lifted one shoulder. "I have intimacy issues. When I slept with women at their houses, I could leave when I wanted to. You're the first girlfriend I ever had who wouldn't take no for an answer."

She turned bright red, looking adorably guilty. "I should probably apologize for that."

He sat on the edge of the bed and put his hand on her ankle, running his hand all the way up to the top of her thigh. Her skin was hot to the touch. "Don't you dare apologize, my feisty little schoolmarm. You saved my life."

Her lashes fluttered closed as he brushed the sensitive folds between her legs. "You were drunk, that's all."

He scooted down in the bed, lifting her ankles to his shoulders, opening her up to his explorations. When he slid two fingers into her moist passage and stroked upward with his thumb, her hips came off the bed. "Devlyn!"

Laughing wickedly, he kissed the place where she glistened, wet and ready for him. "Do you think you're pregnant, Gillian?"

She gasped as he tasted her. "I don't know."

Moving up and over her, he pressed the head of his shaft to the place that was rapidly beginning to feel like home. "Well then, my love, let's hope the third time's a charm."

She sighed, a long, low voluptuous purr that hardened him to the point of pain. "You'll have to give my mother a retirement pension. It would be too weird if she kept working at the castle."

He winced, pausing to glare at her. "Can we please not talk about your mother? Or my father. Or anyone who might happen to be related to either of us? It's putting me off my game."

She dragged down his head for a kiss that was surprisingly erotic for a prim and proper schoolteacher. "Whatever you want, my dear Wolff. Did I ever tell you that triplets run in my family?"

All the air escaped from his lungs in a shell-shocked groan. "Don't even think about it."

Sharp teeth nipped his chin. "All I want to think about is you."

He heard the little gasp that signaled her ultimate pleasure. "Then pay attention, Gillian, because I plan on staying right where I am for the rest of the day."

"Not the night?"

He closed his eyes, thrusting wildly as he climaxed. "That, too," he groaned. "That, too."

* * * * *

REQUEST YOUR FREE BOOKS!

2 FREE NOVELS PLUS 2 FREE GIFTS!

ALWAYS POWERFUL, PASSIONATE AND PROVOCATIVE

YES! Please send me 2 FREE Harlequin Desire® novels and my 2 FREE gifts (gifts are worth about $10). After receiving them, if I don't wish to receive any more books, I can return the shipping statement marked "cancel." If I don't cancel, I will receive 6 brand-new novels every month and be billed just $4.30 per book in the U.S. or $4.99 per book in Canada. That's a saving of at least 14% off the cover price! It's quite a bargain! Shipping and handling is just 50¢ per book in the U.S. and 75¢ per book in Canada.* I understand that accepting the 2 free books and gifts places me under no obligation to buy anything. I can always return a shipment and cancel at any time. Even if I never buy another book, the two free books and gifts are mine to keep forever.

225/326 HDN FEF3

Name _____ (PLEASE PRINT) _____

Address _____ Apt. # _____

City _____ State/Prov. _____ Zip/Postal Code _____

Signature (if under 18, a parent or guardian must sign) _____

Mail to the **Reader Service:**

IN U.S.A.: P.O. Box 1867, Buffalo, NY 14240-1867
IN CANADA: P.O. Box 609, Fort Erie, Ontario L2A 5X3

Not valid for current subscribers to Harlequin Desire books.

Want to try two free books from another line?
Call 1-800-873-8635 or visit www.ReaderService.com.

* Terms and prices subject to change without notice. Prices do not include applicable taxes. Sales tax applicable in N.Y. Canadian residents will be charged applicable taxes. Offer not valid in Quebec. This offer is limited to one order per household. All orders subject to credit approval. Credit or debit balances in a customer's account(s) may be offset by any other outstanding balance owed by or to the customer. Please allow 4 to 6 weeks for delivery. Offer available while quantities last.

HARLEQUIN Blaze
red-hot reads

Two sizzling fairy tales with men straight from your wildest dreams...

Fan-favorite authors

Rhonda Nelson & Karen Foley

bring readers another installment of

Blazing Bedtime Stories, Volume IX

THE EQUALIZER

Modern-day righter of wrongs, Robin Sherwood is a man on a mission and will do everything necessary to see that through, especially when that means catching the eye of a fair maiden.

GOD'S GIFT TO WOMEN

Sculptor Lexi Adams decides there is no such thing as the perfect man, until she catches sight of Nikos Christakos, the sexy builder next door. She convinces herself that she only wants to sculpt him, but soon finds a cold stone statue is a poor substitute for the real deal.

Available October 2012 wherever books are sold.

www.Harlequin.com

HB79715